When the Vow Breaks

BETTY ARRIGOTTI

DEDICATION

For my daughters: Melissa, Theresa, Kathleen, and Jennifer.
My nest may be empty, but you and your daddy continue to fill my
heart.

ACKNOWLEDGMENTS

Montanans tend to exhibit an interesting mix of independence and interdependence. They struggle to do all they can without help, but are at the door with work gloves on whenever someone needs them. I've been the recipient of generous support, from my agent Terry Burns and his editorial assistant, Linda Yezak, to my friends. Brenda listens, Joan keeps me active, and Mary Lou prays with me. To them and all the readers who have encouraged me to keep writing, I say, as they do in Anaconda, "'Preciate it!"

CHAPTER 1

Kay Collie answered her condominium door, and for the first time in her life, passed out.

Before full consciousness returned, the comfort of resting her head against a sturdy shoulder prompted the beginning of a sigh. As she inhaled his scent, her eyes flew open. When she registered the face of the man who carried her toward her couch, rather than over the threshold as he had nineteen years ago, she arched her back and twisted away, fell hard, and struck the back of her head against her coffee table.

"Kay!"

"Don't touch me!" She slapped away his attempt to help her up.

He backed up out of her reach, his hands lifted as if in surrender.

Coward. He must know what she'd like to do to him.

"Are you okay? You scared the daylights out of me when you dropped like that."

As she pushed against the coffee table to stand, black speckles swam before her eyes, and she decided to sit where she was. She lowered her head between her knees. "Why are you here?" Those weren't any of the words she imagined over the years she would say to Wade Hampton, but her head throbbed and those were the best she could do.

"Can I help you up?" He leaned toward her but, at her look, backed away. "I don't know what to do for you."

Eighteen years of child support would be a start, but no way would she tell him that.

"I'll get you a drink." Wade fled to the tiny adjoining kitchen.

Kay wobbled her head to clear it as he returned with a glass of water. She didn't even want to accept that from him. She noticed his diamond studded wedding band. Her hands tightened into fists.

Countless times she had imagined slugging him, kicking him, or slamming a door in his face. Instead she had collapsed at his feet. What a wimp.

He set the glass on the coffee table.

A water drop rolled down the side and she knew it would leave a ring on the wood but she refused to touch the glass. Her jaws didn't unclench as she repeated, "Why are you here?"

Wade lowered himself into the facing chair. He pulled his handkerchief out and slipped it between the glass and the wood. "Can we start over?"

She didn't answer him, so he cleared his throat, and the deep breath he took told her how uneasy he was. Good.

"You look great." His voice held the same tenderness that used to calm all her fears. "You haven't changed."

Kay eased herself onto the edge of the sofa across from him, her back straight, her weight on her toes.

"Of course I've changed. It's been nineteen years. You've changed." He had. Before she had wrenched free, she'd been aware of his strength. He'd filled out since they were eighteen. The extra muscle looked—and felt—good on him. Not that she'd admit it. She studied her feet instead.

"I searched for you." His voice had softened and almost trailed off.

She regarded him openly now. Wade Hampton, in her living room. The touch of grey at his temples surprised her. He was only 37, like her. His eyes looked weary, though kindness still softened their brown depths. She tensed her diaphragm to stop the unbidden internal quiver.

The man had abandoned her, had broken their wedding vows. Yet against all rationale, she still wanted to touch him, to caress away his cares. To go back and undo the mistakes and divulge the secrets.

He had searched for her.

Well, there was that, at least. But he hadn't found her. Until now, when it was too late. She relied on herself now. Her father and Wade had taught her that. She had lived without Wade for too many years, lived in mixed hope and fear.

Hope that he wouldn't give up until he had found her. Fear that when he did his family would take the twins away.

The twins he couldn't know about. Didn't deserve to know about.

Her eyes darted around the room before she calmed herself.

Thank heavens for the strange urge last weekend when she had returned from settling Dana in the dorm to start her first year in college in Seattle. She had collected every picture of the twins into her bedroom to surround herself with them as she tried to sleep her first night in the empty house. Her bedroom door was closed. Another blessing.

She forced herself to refocus on what he was saying.

"I never thought of Spokane. I was sure you would have stayed in Montana for in-state tuition. I knew you wouldn't let go of your dream to be a doctor, but I didn't find you at any of the colleges."

He was wrong. She had given up on becoming a doctor. She had given up everything, and only through sheer willpower had finally managed a career as a nurse. But Dana and Drew made it all worthwhile. Now she'd work every double shift the hospital would offer so that Dana had the chance to live her own dream of a medical degree. Her daughter wouldn't have to scrimp for years and raise two children alone on a nurse's wages.

He looked wistful. "Only 300 miles away all this time." Then his face and voice hardened. "Why did you leave? Why didn't you come back?"

She had her own questions. "How did you find me now?" Why now? Why not all those years ago? What did he want?

"Turns out Mother and Dad knew where you had gone."

She felt a heat rise from her chest to the top of her head and explode into one word. "Wilhelmina!" His mother. The woman who took everything from her.

"I swear I didn't know." Wade spoke rapidly as he stood. "I was furious when Dad admitted last night that they knew all along where you were. They let me waste years in my search for you. But thank God—" He backed away quickly toward the door. Obviously he realized he was not long for this world if he stayed.

"It's your dad… and your mom. They need you to come home."

Her dad? Come home for her dad? Old fears detonated. "Get out! Get out!"

"Kay, calm down. We need to talk."

She stood too quickly and had to steady herself, otherwise she would have lunged at him. "Get out of my house!" She bypassed the glass and grabbed the next thing within reach, a paperback novel. She flung the book at him, and he ducked and stumbled backwards out the door that had been open this whole time. The neighbors would have heard her yelling. Good. Let them call the police.

"Call me after you've calmed down." He fumbled a silver case out of his pocket. "I know it must have been—"

However, Kay had crossed the room and slammed the door, then leaned her back against it.

She slid down the door to the floor and, out of habit, wept silently, though there were no twins in the house to overhear her anymore.

#

Wade tucked his business card under the door and then fled to his royal blue Mustang, the newest in a long line of Mustangs. Aiming the key fob to unlock the door, he glanced back at Kay's condo. Relieved that he couldn't see any of her windows—so she couldn't see him—he dropped into the driver's seat and fought to stem the flood of emotions he had restrained. Starting the engine so he could power down the windows enough to feel fresh air, he forced himself to take deep breaths.

She looked amazing. The nineteen years since they last saw each other hardly touched her. Her waist and hips curved just the same as they used to. Her sweater had given way softly against his chest when he carried her. The remembered sensation caused him to break into a light sweat, and he opened the windows fully. He longed to re-experience her soft lips and glide his fingers through her silky brown hair. Wade squeezed his eyes closed and inhaled deeply.

Man, she looked good. Even when she pelted that book at him. She radiated health.

He couldn't deny the old spark for Kay still glimmered, even after all these years. A dangerous spark he'd have to control when she let him talk to her again.

He shouldn't have come. Time and again he had forced Kay out of his mind, first simply to function and later so he could honor his new marriage vow… But how could he refuse Kay's mother? When he met her in the hall of the hospital, her pain and worry clung to him as tightly as her uninjured hand. She'd begged him to find Kay and bring her home.

He couldn't refuse. He also hadn't thought he'd succeed.

For years, finding Kay to bring her home remained his highest goal. And he had tried. He remembered the first whole summer he searched for her with a black velvet jewelry box that safeguarded the wedding ring in his pocket. Then college started and he traveled to a different state school each break, hoping to find her or someone who knew where she lived. When his investigation turned up no leads, he settled for waiting for her to come home. However, a second summer came and went and she didn't return. Then another. His last hope died when she didn't come back after graduation. That's when he pushed the ring box to the back of his dresser drawer. After law school, he plunged into work in his father's law firm, and left his heart in the drawer with the ring box.

Until Tiffany.

Tiffany. The thought of her hit him like the icy dives during his high school swim season and brought him back under control.

Kay was his past. He had noticed a small wedding band on the same finger where she once wore his class ring. He slid his own wedding ring off his finger and read the inscription again. *"This vow will never be broken."*

Tiffany was his present, and God willing...

He bowed his head. *Dear Jesus, help. I'm trying so hard. I swore I'd never break a wedding vow again. Please, give my wife a new heart. Keep my own heart faithful.*

Wade slid his wedding band onto his finger, stiffened his back, and shifted out of Park. He'd done all he could. He'd handle the rest over the phone when Kay called. Without another glance toward the love of his youth, he drove back to the highway and turned east toward his wife.

#

The next morning Kay awoke grateful for Sunday's escape from the turmoil that constricted her heart. Needing to remind herself she wasn't alone in the world, she dressed for church and hurried to be with people. As she entered the little white-steepled building, she recognized Brenda Potter's salt-and-pepper hair and scooted with relief into the seat beside her friend. Brenda smiled and squeezed Kay's hand. A flood of gratitude threatened Kay's eyes.

After the service, Brenda invited Kay out for breakfast.

"Nonsense," said Kay. "You always come to my place. It's tradition."

"All right, but someday you need to learn how to let others serve you, too."

When Kay had finished her kitchen scurry, they clasped hands and asked for God's blessing over their German pancakes and blackberries.

Brenda held on after the prayer. "Tell me all about it. Did you survive leaving Dana at college, or is she locked up safely in her bedroom?"

Kay's previous dread of empty nesting paled by comparison to what happened yesterday, but Brenda didn't know about her distant past. Was it really only last weekend that she had taken Dana to school? The memory was bright in her mind now. She relived the extended hug outside her daughter's dorm room, then the sense of loss as she left. Loss of her daughter. Loss of her own dream years ago of dorm life and doctor studies.

She forced her mind back to her friend's question and answered, "One daughter's bedroom, almost empty enough to rent out."

"And one mother's empty heart?" Brenda raised her coffee mug to

Kay.

"I'm struggling to focus on this as an opportunity. But, yes, twin holes in this heart."

Brenda set the mug down and grasped Kay's hand in her own again. Kay bowed her head and waited, hoping the prayer she knew was coming would bring comfort and calm. Perhaps Wade would come back today and she would have to face their past once and for all.

"Lord, show Kay the exciting path you've set out for her and give her the courage to follow it."

Kay murmured, "Amen," but felt no ease of her emotions. The two ate in silence until Kay asked, "How did you survive your children moving on?"

"I'd like to say I relied on the Lord for my companionship. Or that my life took on meaning in new ways. I suppose both are true, but it's also true that I mourned some when each child left." Brenda paused to set her fork down and straighten her wedding rings. "Of course, not as much as when their dad passed on. You take comfort in watching your children live their lives." Her voice took on a forced brightness. "What do you hear from Drew?"

"He loves Boot Camp. Happy as can be doing his push-ups in the mud or whatever."

"He's living his dream. I never saw a boy so anxious to serve his country."

"I'm proud of them both."

"You should be. You've done an amazing job raising those two all alone." Brenda slid her plate forward and reached behind her to the counter where she had set her Bible after services.

Kay had often shared this table to study God's word with her friend. She smiled her appreciation for Brenda's words and then waited for whatever Bible verse Brenda wanted to study, still hopeful for a lessening of her loneliness and anger.

Brenda opened the book to the ribbon that saved her place. "This Leviticus passage has intrigued me lately. I'd been reading about how the land and its people were supposed to rest every seventh or Sabbath year, and then I came to this."

She read, turning pronouns to feminine as she often did when she and Kay studied alone, "Consecrate the fiftieth year and proclaim liberty throughout the land to all its inhabitants. It shall be a jubilee for you; each one of you is to return to her family property and each to her own clan."

Return to her family property and each to her own clan. Kay fought a disruption in her soul as if the words plunged roots deep inside her, determined to break through her defenses. She questioned why the excerpt interested Brenda, but she rejected absolutely the admonition to return home. Not now, not ever. The sight of Wade yesterday had ripped open all the old wounds.

She risked blubbering like a fool again if she kept thinking along these lines. She focused on her friend and smiled at the light in Brenda's eyes and the excitement in her voice.

"This passage ignites something in me. I'm almost fifty and it's making me want to commemorate my jubilee year. It goes on to talk about celebration, declaration of freedom, forgiveness of debts… I don't know how yet, but I'm going to celebrate! Will you help me?"

Kay remembered her tentative steps into the church five years earlier when Drew's early teen years had sent her to her knees. Brenda appointed herself Kay's welcome committee that first day. From then on, this dear friend showered love on the twins as if they were her own.

"Of course I'll help. What are you thinking?"

"I want to give a party to honor turning fifty, becoming a jubilee woman!"

Brenda pulled a pen and pad from the purse at her feet and started writing notes. Kay watched, happy to see her friend so excited, but also struggling to unknot her abdominal muscles. She refused to examine her visceral reaction to the reading.

The older woman stopped and looked up, a sheepish expression replacing the light in her eyes. She set her pen down. "I'm sorry. I got carried away by the Word there. You didn't get to respond to it. What struck you in the reading?"

Kay didn't want to answer. Though the words obviously energized Brenda, Kay still battled the adrenaline they shot through her own nervous system.

Brenda sat, waited, and appeared quite contrite.

Kay glanced down and swallowed to loosen a tightening in her throat. She clasped her hands together to keep them from shaking. "Return to family. I only heard, 'return to her family.' Everything else faded out." She had lived more years away from home than she had lived there. Wilhelmina had made going home impossible, even if she wanted to, which she didn't.

Brenda laid her hand over Kay's. "You've never talked about your childhood. What does the passage mean to you?"

Brenda's hand felt warm, but Kay drew hers away. "I don't know. And I don't want to know."

"Kay, sometimes we realize a message is meant for us because it brings a sense of joy, like this did for me. Other times the words shake our very foundations, they sound so hard. When they do that, I think God is asking us to trust Him."

Kay sighed. "Your joy sounds more fun." Definitely time for a subject change. "What were you writing?"

Brenda peered over her glasses at Kay, but didn't push. "I started jotting a list of all the women who've been important to my life. I'm going to invite every one of them to my party to thank them. I'll call them my jubilee women." She closed her Bible, but rested her hand on the cover. "I've lived seven Sabbath years. I didn't spend any seventh year setting aside work or forgiving debts or consecrating it to God, but I'm determined to do something special for my jubilee year. Now, since you are on the top of the list, when shall we have it?"

Kay laughed, relieved to be diverted from the heaviness that first Wade and now these words had placed on her soul. She never could have taken off work for a year every seventh year, nor even rested one day a week. Though the twins were gone, she'd have to work as hard as ever to pay Dana's tuition. This message couldn't apply to single mothers. She didn't need to go back home.

This was Brenda's message of celebration. Helping her plan a party, that Kay could manage. A party would distract her from empty-nest loneliness.

Brenda's face brightened. "I'll give a tea to thank the women who've influenced me. Beautiful flowers and some kind of homemade favors. Oh! I want chocolate-dipped strawberries and little tea cakes...."

After the two had written lists of people to invite, party favors to consider, and food to prepare, Kay saw her friend to the door.

Brenda hugged her. "Don't worry about your reaction to our reading today, Kay. You'll know what God wants from you, and He'll give you strength to do it."

Kay nodded, but mentally she shook her head and stamped her foot. If God wanted her to return home, it would take a lightning bolt or a personal visit from an angel to talk her into it.

Wade was no angel, yet his business card tugged at her conscience.

CHAPTER 2

"Wade Hampton speaking."

Wade's voice still stirred something within her, even after all these years.

"All right. I'm listening. Tell me what you came to say." Kay had surrendered. For hours, the words from the Bible had replayed in her mind. *Each one of you is to return to her family...* She couldn't go home but she could call Wade and hear him out.

Wade paused a moment, and then his words poured out and pummeled her. "Kay, I came for your mom. She's in the hospital. She begged me to find you and bring you home."

"Mom needs me?" She must have misunderstood when he mentioned her dad the day before. Her mom needed her. Not her dad.

"Your father—I don't know what you know—he had a stroke way back after you left. She's been taking care of him for years. Last night he collapsed—another stroke they think—and she fell trying to help him, or maybe he fell on her. Her shoulder's broken. He might be dying." His voice took on urgency. "Kay, they need you to come home."

The jolt in Kay's chest felt like a hypodermic needle plunge. She imagined a cardiac patient's response while her own heart raced. Kay's worst fears growing up had come true. Her dad had put her mother in the hospital. Wade said he might be dying. She refused to feel guilty for the years of wishing him dead.

Every nerve in her body wanted to decline, but God seemed to want her to go. And her mother, she should go for her mother.

However, she had promised Wilhelmina not to return. One thing Kay would never do is break a promise. Still, Wade said his parents told him how to find her. They must be releasing her from what Wilhelmina had made her swear.

As soon as she mumbled her assent, Wade said a quick goodbye and hung up. The questions that she would have liked to ask him, the things she long imagined saying to him, had to be postponed.

She needed to pack. Call work. Hurry.

Her mother needed her, but Kay struggled yet again to accept that Wade did not. How she had longed for Wade to need her, to want her to come back.

Kay grabbed a few changes of clothes and threw her small suitcase into the back of her car. As she gripped the steering wheel, she noticed her wedding ring and groaned. But what did it matter that Wade must have seen it? He obviously had no interest in her. He'd remarried. How many times had she repeated those words over the years? Still, she slid the ring off and plunged it into her purse before beginning her drive.

After five hours driving through valleys and mountain passes while arguing herself out of turning around, she read the "Welcome to Butte, Montana" sign. She clenched the wheel. She could do this. She would get her mother set up with whatever help she needed and be out of town without Wade finding out about the twins.

Even in the dusk of evening, every block showed evidence of economic downturn—dented cars, empty storefronts, and pot-holed streets. An occasional business seemed to boast success, but many needed upkeep far beyond a coat of paint. Black tripod mine frames silhouetted against the darkening sky and grey leaves blowing across the street intensified the bleak atmosphere. At this mile-high altitude, winter overpowered autumn well before its time.

The hospital lot was full, so Kay found a parking place on a nearby street and turned the wheels against the curb. The hills of Butte defied any brake to hold against such odds. Once in the six-story brick building, a slight smell of Lysol drew her back in time. Her mother had spent her life washing these floors to keep the three of them fed and warm and that smell had clung to her clothes. The familiar resentment rose as Kay thought of her father and the many ways he failed them.

She stopped at the information desk.

"I'm Kay Collie. I'm here for Sadie Collie.... And Stu." She cringed inside as she spoke her father's name. How many times had children teased about her dad being stewed, marinated in the juice of his six packs?

"Shoot, Kay-girl! People wondered if this'd be enough to bring you home!" The receptionist seemed familiar in spite of her neon orange hair, but Kay hadn't thought about most of the people of her past for so long that she couldn't place her.

"You remember me. Francie Winters. Francie Shea now. I was your biology partner sophomore year. Sorry about your folks, girl." She pointed to the elevator. "You better see your dad first. He's in ICU on third floor. Your mom's having more tests right now."

"Thanks, Francie." Kay gave the fact that she had no memory of sophomore biology class only a quick thought before she turned her attention to Francie's recommendation to see her father first. Her mom's need had brought Kay back to her past. Her dad didn't deserve attention.

Honor thy father and thy mother. Her conscience forced her feet toward the intensive care unit where she was directed to his curtained cubicle. She scanned the monitors behind the bed before compelling herself to look at him.

The man lying there held little resemblance to the towering, large-fisted father who had inspired only bitterness and fear in his daughter. Frail and thin, his breath measured time in short gasps. Despite her reluctance, she moved to the side of the bed. The motion woke him and he looked up at her. A weak, crooked smile lit one side of his face. The other side remained still, and Kay had an eerie feeling that half the man's body was dead and the other half would follow soon.

"Kay." His voice rasped, but his mind must be intact. He knew her. His right hand lay curled and motionless on his blanket, but he raised his left hand toward her.

She drew back, an automatic reaction from the past, and he let his hand fall.

"I'm sorry," he whispered.

Kay had never heard him whisper. He boomed, he growled, he slurred, but he never whispered.

"Where's..." She leaned in to catch his words. "...Mother?"

She hated that he called his wife that. She didn't remember him ever calling her Sadie. Certainly no endearments. "Mother, bring a beer!" were the most common words from his mouth.

"She okay?" His voice sounded childlike in his concern.

Touched, though she didn't want to be, Kay answered. "I don't know, Dad. I just got here, but I'll go find out."

"Kay," he stopped her. "Sorry... hurt you."

She fled the room; this slight remnant of her father who smiled and apologized and lay helpless in his bed proved too much of a contradiction to the villain of her past.

In the hallway, a gurney rattled toward her. She averted her eyes from the white haired lady, thinking to give her privacy, but the woman murmured, "Kay."

Startled, Kay beheld a faded, wrinkled version of her mother.

"Mama!" As the attendant paused his advance, she bent to hug Sadie Collie.

"Careful, dear. Left shoulder hurts something awful." Her eyes attested to the pain, so Kay held Sadie's right hand, instead.

"You saw your father?"

Kay nodded, overcome by the infirmity of both parents. Her hope for a quick return to Spokane dwindled.

"Good, good. I know it was hard for you to come. Now, go get them to assign me to the same room as him." She lifted her chin to see the orderly. "Ben, you might as well wheel me to Stu. Kay's here. She's going to make everything right."

"Ok, Sadie, you're the boss." He shrugged at Kay.

Kay sighed and headed for the nurses' station. She was here, but she doubted God himself could make everything right in her family.

When Kay returned to the ICU, her mother's bed nestled against the side of her father's. Sadie's good hand clasped Stu's. Kay had never seen such tenderness between them before. Both parents slept, so Kay slipped out, hoping for a moment alone to gather her emotions. Turning into the hallway, she stopped short. For the second time in two days, Wade stood in front of her.

"I'm glad you came, Kay." The gentle brown eyes hinted at a smile, but his look of weariness and sadness overshadowed any pleasure he showed in seeing her. She realized with a start that his need for solace might rival her own. Of course he was tired. He had traveled 300 miles and back yesterday to bring her news of her parents. She could at least be civil.

"Are you all right, Wade?" But at his look of discomfort, she hurried to keep him from having to answer. "Thank you for telling me about my folks. I wouldn't have known until I saw it in the paper." She pressed her lips together, too late.

He stood straighter. "You get the Standard sent to Spokane?"

The questions that drove her to distraction during her long drive poured out. "How did your parents find me? How long have they known where I live? Why didn't you come years ago?"

Did he always know, but not care to see her? She hadn't changed her name, both hoping and afraid he would seek her out, but the years had passed and she figured he hadn't tried. *He's married to someone else*, she reminded herself, as she had so many times before.

"Dad knew somehow you worked at Sacred Heart Hospital. He never told me until two nights ago when Sadie asked me to find you."

"But you came to my home."

"I told the lady at the Sacred Heart information desk about your folks. She called you but didn't get an answer so she gave me your address." He paused, then seemed to draw courage. "Kay, have you been happy?"

Kay considered how to answer him, but a high-pitched alarm from the ICU cut all thought short. She rushed into the room to find her mother struggling to sit up, such fright twisting her features that Kay reached out to hold her. But her mother pushed her aside and stretched her good arm toward her husband. Kay studied her father as the code signal registered from her years of nursing experience. Stu's heart had stopped. Hurried footsteps approached, but no crash cart? Where was the defibrillator?

Her mother cried, "Stu, no! Not now! Kay's here at last!"

Kay stepped aside to let a doctor gain access to her father. He scowled when he saw the two beds filling the cramped space but hurried to listen through his stethoscope at the man's chest. He stood back. Why wasn't he doing more to revive him? Then she realized her father must have prohibited resuscitation in an advance directive.

"I'm sorry, Mrs. Collie," the doctor said. "He's gone." He turned and added, "I'm glad you were finally here, Kay. I hope you had a chance to say goodbye."

What did he mean, finally here? Her father's stroke was only 2 nights ago. And how did he know her name? Kay glanced at his ID and realization dawned. Jim Kelly. A younger version of this doctor had been a year behind her in high school. Did the whole town know how long she had been gone? The circumstances of her leaving?

Sadie wept softly. Kay couldn't cry for her father, but she would do what she could to comfort her mother. She drew close to Sadie's bed and stroked the age-spotted hand gently. "I'm sorry you're so sad, Mama." She had always regretted the unhappiness of her mother's life, but the worst was over now. Mama's tormentor had died. So why did her mother sound like her heart was broken?

Kay glanced up. Wade stood at the doorway, watching. As their eyes met, he turned and hurried away.

Now Kay cried, too. Were the tears for the father Stu should have been and never would be? Or for watching Wade leave her again?

CHAPTER 3

Wade hurried back toward the elevator, his fists and teeth clenched. He hadn't meant to intrude, simply to check and see if Kay had made it to town. He should have insisted she listen to him yesterday and then offered to have her ride with him. What kind of man would tell a woman on the phone that her father might be dying, her mother seriously injured, and then let her drive herself across three states to the hospital?

Wade berated himself for not inviting her, not considering her needs. Although if he had, the thought of spending five hours with her beside him in a car... Not a good idea. And the wedding ring he'd seen on her finger was now gone. Why wasn't her husband here to comfort her?

He pushed the button and waited for the elevator.

The scene he had glimpsed from outside the doorway of the ICU froze in his mind. The way Kay comforted her mother with such love. The look on her face when she saw him. Then the pain that registered there, almost as if he caused it. No, she abandoned her feelings for him when she left town. She must have been grieving for her father. Poor Kay. She had come home too late to know the good man Stu Collie had become.

The elevator doors opened and he stepped inside. He nodded to the beaming young man and smiled at the young woman in the wheelchair. But she didn't notice him. She was gazing into the eyes of her newborn.

Kay's grief. He understood that emotion. He pictured himself in that young man's place, his hand resting on the wheelchair, Tiffany sitting next to him, held rapt by their son. He imagined himself leaning down to kiss their baby and then her. But the face that lifted to receive his kiss was Kay's. He shook his head to clear it, and the bell dinged. He stepped through the elevator doors to the second floor and listened to them close on what might have been.

Wade pushed open the door of room 202. Tiffany glanced away from the television. "You were gone a long time for a cup of coffee."

"Did you need something?"

"Yeah, a new heart. Did you find one?"

A light knock on the door announced his mother's entrance into the room, carrying several magazines. Wade doubted anyone else still dressed up for hospital visits, but he knew his mother would have changed before coming. She appeared as elegant as always.

"Hello, Mother. Nice of you to come." Tiffany's bed was between him and his mother, so he nodded and smiled, rather than offer their usual stilted hug.

"Hello, dear. Tiffany, you look like you might be up to paging through some of these magazines. We'll need your ideas for the fashion show next month."

Tiffany smiled and motioned for Wilhelmina to set them down on the bedside table. Her short blond hair once shone in any light but now lay dull against her pillow. Her high cheekbones that used to glow pink without makeup had lost their color. He hoped his mother was right, that soon his wife would be back to work with her on their never-ending fundraisers, but seeing the pallor of her skin, he found it hard to believe. Looking back at Wilhelmina, he noticed a shadow of doubt cross her face before she blinked and resumed her too cheery smile.

She turned toward him. "Where were you all day yesterday, Wade? I tried calling your house."

"Business, Mom." His own business. He hadn't told her or Tiffany about his drive to and from Spokane. His father knew and that was bad enough. Tiffany would never understand.

#

Two hours later, Wade kissed Tiffany goodnight on the forehead and deaded to his dark, empty house. Before he faced his lonely bedroom, he selected a photo album off the bookshelf in his study. He sat on the brown leather side chair and paged through the picture account of his seven years of marriage to Tiffany. She was a beautiful, glowing bride. He looked the part of a serious young lawyer.

He turned a page. His mother and his wife stood arm-in-arm at some formal function. They'd grown close, those two. Tiffany became his mother's acolyte, accepting instruction in all social responsibilities. She even adopted Wilhelmina's imperious tone of voice. He cringed at the thought and turned the page quickly.

Between thumb and forefinger of each hand, Tiffany pinched a tiny T-shirt with the words, "Grandma's gonna love me." Their happiness had been so brief. The next page held no picture, only pressed flower petals from the bouquet he had brought to the hospital when she miscarried. He turned the page again and Tiffany was blowing out candles on her 27th birthday, the circles under her eyes remnants of her first heart attack. How could anyone so young be so sick?

Wade rested his elbows on the album pages, his hands clasped together as if hanging on to a rope. He had wanted to comfort her and draw comfort from her, but she turned him away saying, "I need you to move to another bedroom."

He had laughed at first. "Tiffany, the doctor said after a few weeks it would be fine for us to be intimate again."

But she remained too frightened. After days of reasoning, pleading, and—he was embarrassed to remember—shouting, he had given in. He thought it wouldn't last long. She would miss him and invite him back.

In five years, she hadn't.

More photos showed that they had remained publicly affectionate. He consoled himself that they were close in other respects. She regaled him with funny accounts of her fundraising adventures and listened to his stories about work. They spent quiet evenings together and, when she was well, often went out to a movie or dinner. But they lived as friends and never again as lovers.

Wade replaced the book and turned out the light. He climbed the stairs and opened the door to Tiffany's room. He would accept it all if she could be healthy and home again. But this time, the empty bed had waited longer than any other hospital stay.

In his room, he stepped out of his pants and pulled off his shirt. His own heart proved too weary for him to do more than climb into his bed. Too tired to do the blood sugar test he knew he should. He prayed, as he did every night, for strength to remain steadfast to his vows.

#

After Stu Collie's death, a nurse gave Kay's mother a sedative that ushered her into merciful sleep. Kay, however, would have to wait for her chance to rest.

The nurse guided her back to orange-haired Francie, where paperwork needed her signature. Decisions and arrangements must be made. With her mother scheduled tomorrow for shoulder replacement, days would pass before she'd be released from the hospital, and weeks before she could live alone. Kay realized she would need to stay at least long enough to find live-in help for her mother.

"You should call her church." Francie seemed to sense Kay was overwhelmed by the sudden demands of the situation. "The office is closed now, but in the morning they could help you."

"Mom has a church?" Kay's dad had always refused to allow either of them to attend.

"Yes, Our Savior's, down on Park Street. I see her there every week. In fact, why don't I call tomorrow and have someone meet you at your folks' place?"

A shiver shook her shoulders. Kay hadn't considered stepping foot back in her parents' house. But it would save money needed for Dana's college if she could stay there for the time being, rather than in a motel. Years of stretching her finances to fit the needs of a family of three made the decision automatic. Still, it wouldn't do to have anyone come to her parents' home and see the way they lived.

"Could you ask them to come here instead? I want to spend as much time with Mom as I can."

Kay walked to her car and drove to the house, feeling like a prisoner dragged toward a dungeon. In less than five minutes, her headlights lit the little grey, two-story house that had witnessed her childhood. The yard seemed larger than she remembered it. No broken-down cars overflowed the driveway, awaiting her father's random attempts to repair them, inspired when his alcohol supply ran low. No weeds competed to hide tires or engine blocks. In fact, from what she could tell in the dark, both the yard and the house looked better cared for than she could ever recall.

Kay remembered Wade's words about her father suffering a stroke soon after she left. How had her parents' lives changed after that?

She tried the front door and, finding it locked, realized she should have asked for her father's belongings when she left the hospital in case she needed his keys. She picked her way through the dark to the back of the house, carrying the suitcase she had packed after her phone call to Wade earlier that afternoon. His visit seemed long ago and her Spokane home far away. She had managed less than a week in her empty nest.

The back door opened without the creaking she anticipated. Her hand moved to the light switch, muscle memory from years past. The pink kitchen she entered appeared much like it always had, though tidier. She propped her suitcase against the table, then approached the living room. The swinging door that used to divide the two rooms was gone. Again, she could switch on the light without fumbling, but that was the last familiarity Kay felt.

This room bore no resemblance to the living room of her youth. With a start, she wondered if she was in the right house. Her parents might have moved since she left. She might be in someone else's home, someone who could be asleep upstairs. She considered sneaking out, but then caught sight of a picture of herself, taken her senior year. Its smile didn't reach the wary eyes but the photo proved she was in the right home.

She exhaled and studied the room again. Instead of the recliner, sofa, and television that had dominated the room, her parents' bed stood against the far stair wall. The bed was unmade and a nightstand lay on its side nearby. The telephone must have fallen to the floor during the episode that brought her parents to the hospital, one suffering from stroke and the other with a broken shoulder. Kay imagined the scene and whispered a quick prayer of thanks that the phone landed within reach.

Kay drew her attention away from that corner, feeling she had invaded an area of privacy. An easel and paint supplies claimed the front window, and two overstuffed rockers snuggled near each other across from it. When had her mother begun to paint? She walked to the window and caught her breath. Several beautiful portraits leaned against the easel. She flipped through them and stopped at an unfinished one.

Her chest tightened and her nose tingled. She blinked away tears that blurred the face—her face—that stared back at her, a lovely copy of her senior picture: chestnut hair, green eyes specked with yellow, a slightly crooked nose ridge, above lips she had always thought too thin but that the artist had curved into a determined, hope-filled smile.

"Oh, Mama, you've captured my feeling that day more beautifully than the photograph. Wade and I were happy, the future promising...." How she wished she could go back to that time and redo her choices. And his.

The face appeared completed but her shoulders and dress were only sketched. It struck Kay as fitting that her portrait waited, in progress. Her life itself, her little family, her hopes for the future had always felt incomplete. Still, once her mother returned home, maybe she would paint in the details. Kay slid her portrait under the easel clamps, hoping it would be her mother's first project.

She moved to the two blue rockers. Their worn upholstery and dipping seats showed years of use. To the side of one, a basket held soft navy yarn and a half-finished knitting project. She sat in her mother's chair and studied the room around her, amazed at how life had changed in a matter of hours.

She marveled even more at how her life had developed from when she lived in this house. She smiled and squared her shoulders. Two children, a career, and a happy life that she had built from so little. Yet, this room spoke of the changes in the lives of those she left behind. The ever-present tension in the air was gone. Creativity happened here, and Kay could sense its healing effects.

Sitting still, Kay acknowledged her weariness. She rose and retrieved her suitcase from the kitchen. Returning to the living room, she passed through it to the tiny entry. Near the front door on her right, a folded wheelchair leaned against the wall. She regarded it a moment, then turned left and climbed the stairs to her old room.

The metamorphosis of the living room did not extend this far. Her room remained like the day she left it. Her little twin bed still wore the lavender bedspread that she had purchased with babysitting money. Someone, no doubt her mother, had dusted the mismatched desk and dresser recently. She smiled to see the textbooks from her senior year lined against the wall at the back of the desk. The photo of Wade on the dresser proved more than she could handle. She turned it face down, but stroked the frame's felt backing.

Kay opened the door to her closet. Hardly any clothes remained where her shirts and dresses had hung. Her mother had kept a small number of sentimental reminders: the light blue dress Sadie helped her make for her first formal dance with Wade, the high school jacket he gave her, complete with his letter from swim team, and her burgundy senior prom dress. To the left of the hanging clothes, favorite books and toys still lined the shelves. A teddy bear, a baby doll. Her all-time favorite doll, of course, was missing. She cringed, remembering the way its china head shattered during one of her father's rages.

She jerked the string to turn off the closet light and set to work getting ready for bed.

Once during the night she awoke from a dream of a younger Wade, and was suddenly hyper-alert to the sounds of the house settling. She listened, out of old habit, in case her father's footsteps on the stairs might drum the warning of his drunken anger. Then she remembered he never again would climb those steps, slam open her mother's door, and take out the shame of his failures on his wife. Or his daughter.

But Wade could never again comfort her the way he used to, either.

CHAPTER 4

Kay rose early that Monday and by sunrise she sat in the surgery waiting room, praying for a successful operation that would ease her mother's pain. She asked for guidance on the decisions that lay ahead and wondered if it was wrong to pray that she could get back to work quickly. With her head bowed, she ignored the sounds of someone's approach until two sensible shoes clomped into her peripheral vision.

"Kay Collie?"

Kay looked up. "Yes?"

"I'm Madge Pike."

The woman's air gave Kay the impression she should apologize for something. She rose to stand level with her accuser and waited for further explanation.

"I'm on the hospitality committee at Our Savior."

Heaven help the hospitality committee, Kay thought.

"How's your mother?" Madge's features softened a bit, as did her voice, but Kay suspected it was not for her benefit. "I'm sorry about your dad."

"Mom's in surgery. Her shoulder broke in the fall." How much did Madge, or for that matter, the town, know? Probably more than she did herself.

"Your mother's a saint." The tone made it clear that Madge had no such misconceptions about Kay.

Kay nodded. She doubted this sensible-shoed woman had any idea what their life had entailed, but from childhood Kay knew not to discuss the failings of her father, nor the sufferings of her mother.

"So how did they find you? Your mother never knew where you lived." A raised chin emphasized the indictment.

Kay held her gaze, refusing to divulge what was private.

Madge harrumphed. "I talked to Reverend Rob. He can do a memorial service for your father at ten on Thursday at the church."

"I don't know if Mom will be released from the hospital by then. I won't do it without her." Kay lifted her own chin.

Madge's eyes welled, taking Kay completely by surprise. "You're right. Won't ever seem right to see Sadie in church without Stu."

Kay cocked her head, straining to decipher Madge's words. "Dad went to church with Mom?"

"Every week! Often on Wednesday evenings, too. She'd roll him right up to the front pew, park him in the aisle, and squeeze past him to sit in the pew next to him. The building committee even talked about shortening the pew so he wouldn't have to sit in the aisle." She shook her head slowly. "But then we wouldn't be able to see them holding hands all through the service. Too late now, I suppose."

Kay squeezed her eyes closed. The mental image was more than she could fathom. "How long have they been going to church?"

"Quite a testimony, theirs. Stu's first stroke changed their lives for the better. Not that you—"

"Kay Collie?" A man approached them as he pulled a fresh scrubs shirt over his undershirt. His handshake exuded confidence. "Ken Cohen." His words came clipped and decisive. "Your mom's surgery went well, but we did need to replace the shoulder joint. She's going to require pain medication for quite a while during recovery. She won't be able to raise her arm for several weeks, so she'll need someone to live with her."

He paused as if to let her catch up. "Can you arrange it? Otherwise she'll transfer from here to the nursing home until she can take care of herself again."

Madge interrupted Kay's effort to comprehend the implication of the doctor's orders. "I don't suppose Kay can take much time from whatever kept her away this long. The ladies at church will do what we can."

"I don't need help. I'll stay!"

The look on Madge's face registered no less surprise than Kay felt herself, yet the effect gave her a moment of pleasure. She leaned forward and eyed Madge steadily. "I'm here now, and I'll stay for as long as my mother needs me. You ladies won't need to trouble yourselves."

The doctor broke the tension. "I'll check on Sadie in the morning. She'll remain in recovery for another hour or so, and then you can see her back in her room."

Kay's shoulders relaxed. Madge shrugged and left without a word.

Kay's sense of victory drained away. She slumped back into her seat, mentally listing all the phone calls she needed to make.

Dana. Drew. How much did each have to know?

The hospital in Spokane. This would count as sick leave, but without overtime how would she make the college payment?

#

Kay felt drained emotionally, but once her mother returned from recovery and fell asleep, one unpleasant task remained. Wishing she could be headed anywhere else, she drove to the funeral home.

An overpowering floral scent greeted her even before a Southern gentleman's, "May I help you?"

She remembered his face but not his name. She had thought him ancient when he directed Wade's sister's funeral. He must be in his nineties now. But he still carried himself with dignity and spoke in a comforting murmur.

"I'm Kay Collie."

He patted her hand while he shook it. "Of course, Miss Collie. I am sorry about your father. I first met Mr. Collie about ten years ago. What a gentle man."

Gentle was not how she would have described her father, but Kay didn't want to encourage more discussion. She simply needed to make the necessary arrangements and get back to her mother. Or better yet, drive to Spokane, climb into her bed, and pull the covers over her head for a week.

She followed Mr. Fellow—she would have gotten his name eventually but the nametag made it easier—into his office where he selected a file from the cabinet. "Your father foresaw this day and made arrangements four or five years ago. He didn't want Miss Sadie having to fuss with these things."

Kay felt some of the tension in her shoulders ease. If he'd made arrangements already, this should be quick.

"Please follow me, and I'll show you his choices."

"Oh, that won't be—" but it seemed Mr. Fellow was a bit hard of hearing, because he continued to shuffle toward another room. Kay took a deep breath and followed. The heavy florist-shop smell gave way to the aroma of cedar when they entered a room with dozens of caskets. Some shone gold, bronze, or silver, but those built of beautiful woods attracted her most. Kay passed a small white casket, and the thought of a child's death nearly brought her to tears. The mortician stopped at a mahogany casket and opened it to show the rich red velvet lining.

24

"When will the service be taking place?" he asked.

"We haven't set a date yet. My mother is still in the hospital, and I want to be sure she'll be recovered enough to attend." Kay ran her hand along the glossy wood. "This is beautiful."

"Yes, your father had artistic taste. It's a fine model, and not unreasonably priced. Dignified without extravagance. Sometimes families spend more than they should afford, trying to express the love they feel. Mr. Collie didn't want Miss Sadie to be put in that position."

He stared down at his feet, then at Kay. "Forgive me for asking, but when do you expect your mother to be able to attend?"

"I'd guess at least a couple of weeks before she's up to this. Is that a problem?"

"Oh dear." Mr. Fellow looked down at the form with her father's arrangements. "We make every effort to follow the wishes of the departed, but on occasion circumstances don't allow…"

He closed the file folder. "Miss Collie, I'd advise a cremation. That way the remains will wait until your mother is ready. I'm sure we can find an urn made of this same wood. Then you may choose to deposit the urn in the plot your father chose or in our columbarium vault."

Kay's relief that her father had made these decisions evaporated. She must choose to go against his wishes or have Sadie miss the service. Well, she wouldn't attend his memorial service without her mother. She felt a tiny thrill at thwarting her father's plans, then reprimanded herself, and added guilt to her skirmishing emotions.

Mr. Fellow smiled kindly. "The details of services and burials are for the benefit of the living. I'm sure your father nods from heaven, wanting you and Miss Sadie to choose what's best for you. He understands."

Kay wondered if the elderly gentleman was reassuring himself, as much as her. "You're right, Mr. Fellow. Thank you."

They chose a mahogany urn, and Kay left, relieved to have the ordeal behind her. She couldn't, however, shake free of an image of her father outside the heavenly gates, beer can in hand and leaning against a rusty car. That night she dreamed the scene, but her father tossed the beer can away, pulled on a black suit coat, and sat down in a wheelchair. He smiled and waved at Kay, then rolled through the gates. When Kay awoke in the morning, the smile and wave irritated her more than the beer can.

#

Kay called Brenda before returning to the hospital. Her friend's voice bounced from worry to relief to excitement. "Kay, where are you? I tried calling you several times yesterday. I'm like a little girl again, planning my Jubilee party! I could hardly sleep last night thinking of all the details."

"Oh, Brenda, that Bible verse. Yesterday I swore I'd never return home like it said. Today I'm sitting in the house where I grew up." She caught Brenda up to date, which wasn't easy since she had never talked about life before Spokane.

"God's certainly at work. I'm sorry about your dad. How did your mom's surgery go?"

"I should be heading to her right now. Brenda, I'm going to need to stay here to help until Mom's able to be alone. Could you use the spare key I gave you and forward my phone to—" She glanced down at the rotary dial and changed her mind. "I'll call you once I buy a cell phone and give you the number."

"Do the twins know?" The concern in Brenda's voice comforted Kay.

"I don't want them to, yet. I need to think this all through. It's happening too fast."

"Then I'll pray for your wisdom and God's consolation."

Kay knew Brenda's words weren't empty. She had often prayed with her through her friend's long list of people's intentions. Brenda continued to pray daily about each problem until she learned of its resolution.

Kay gave up second-guessing herself about her next request. "This will sound strange, Brenda, but I need to ask a favor. Could you wrap and send me the large framed photo of me holding the babies that's usually on the living room wall. It's in my bedroom now."

After Brenda wrote down the Butte address she said goodbye, adding, "I'm not having my party until you're back. Hurry home!"

The portrait would be a comfort to her in the days ahead, even if no one else could be allowed to see it. However, she admitted to herself that the document that hid behind the picture in the frame was what she truly needed. That paper had become her security blanket. Keeping it close soothed her lonely soul.

#

Kay kept vigil at her mother's side in room 305 most of that day. The drugs' effects had eased, and Sadie seemed more alert, though she still slept much of the time. During one of the naps, Kay ventured to the cafeteria for a quick sandwich. Wade sat at a table staring at the mug his hands enfolded. Looking up, he saw Kay and stood. "Join me?"

His voice carried pleasure at seeing her, but then his face clouded. She nodded, went to select her meal, and then returned.

"You come here often?" She didn't suppose he was hanging around the hospital hoping to see her, but she couldn't figure why a lawyer would spend so much time here. He certainly had too much class to be an ambulance chaser looking for clients. She set down her tray and took a seat. "Is someone sick?" Her heart skipped a beat. He didn't look healthy. "Are you all right?"

He swallowed hard and fixed his gaze at a point beyond her.

Kay glanced over her shoulder, but no one was there.

"What is it, Wade?"

"Tiffany." His eyes shot back and forth between Kay and the cafeteria entrance. "I shouldn't be— I need to get back to her." He stood and his chair nearly fell backwards.

She watched him hurry to the elevator and punch the button repeatedly. She had hated the name Tiffany ever since she read about his marriage in the Standard.

Francie, the receptionist, set her tray down at Kay's table. "Don't mind him. Okay to sit, or do you want to be alone?"

Kay motioned for her to join her. "What's wrong with Tiffany?"

"Not supposed to discuss the patients, you know." She placed her napkin carefully on her lap. "Not that it's a secret. Everybody in town knows Tiffany's waiting for a heart transplant."

Kay felt her neck and cheeks warm. She was shocked at her own mixed feelings. "How awful!" she managed, afraid her words rang hollow.

"It is. I know you and Wade were a thing in high school. But you left, and he grieved over you for years. Then Tiffany fell for him and he came alive again. She was good for him, at least for a while."

Kay's sigh was audible, and Francie reached over and laid her hand on Kay's. "Must be hard coming back and knowing people judge you. I remember in biology how sad you felt about inflicting pain on a chick. Remember giving them those injections? I know you wouldn't have hurt Wade or your folks on purpose. I always figured you had serious reasons. I'm glad to see you back, though."

Kay did remember Francie now, and her struggles through their science classes. Kay had befriended her after noticing the way Francie flinched if someone passed behind her. She suspected they had more in common than biology.

"So, 'Francie Winters, now Francie Shea,' how's married life?"

Francie stopped lifting her sandwich toward her mouth, looked straight into Kay's eyes and then nodded, as if coming to a decision. "We're not living together. Haven't been for four years now."

Kay felt the flush of her face intensify. "Oh, Francie. I'm sorry. You probably don't want to talk about it."

"Actually, it might do me good. People here think they know the story, so never bring it up. I'm still trying to come to grips with it myself."

"You're divorced?"

She shrugged her shoulders. "Neither of us ever filed, though I can't imagine why he hasn't." She set her sandwich down and leaned back in her chair. Kay took a sip of her coffee and waited.

"You know what it's like living with an alcoholic, right?"

Kay would never get used to it. People saying aloud what she had barely admitted to herself. But she guessed Francie would be the last to judge. She nodded.

"You'd think with dads like ours we'd never touch a drop of alcohol, but some of us don't learn from other's mistakes. By the time I graduated from high school, I was binge drinking every weekend. So was Allen, my boyfriend then."

Kay was surprised but decided she shouldn't have been. Weekend parties were common when she was in high school, but she hadn't gone to any. They weren't part of her plans to be a doctor.

"I finished beauty school and was working at a hair salon and Allen got a job in Anaconda working for his brother-in-law. After a few years of working days and drinking nights, I got pregnant, Allen proposed, and we got married. He turned his life around, determined to be a good husband and dad. I didn't."

Francie glanced at her watch, said, "Shoot," and took a big bite of her sandwich. After she swallowed, she shrugged. "I have to get back. Maybe we can catch up more soon. You haven't told me anything about where you've been and what you've been doing, and I've only covered my first years out of high school." She took another bite and raised her eyebrows in a wordless apology.

Francie's need to return to work relieved Kay's tension. She didn't want to share about her past, and the warm compliment of having someone confide in her might have led her to reciprocate more than she should.

They finished their meals quickly and then rode the elevator together toward their respective responsibilities, but the words "waiting for a heart transplant" reverberated louder in Kay's mind than Francie's admission or their elevator small talk.

CHAPTER 5

Sadie roused as Kay entered. The memory of her mother and father holding hands across their beds in ICU made this private room seem lonely. Kay settled into the chair next to the bed and her mother smiled.

"I keep opening my eyes to make sure your coming wasn't a dream."

"Nope, I'm here, Mom." She studied the bedspread. "I'm sorry it took me so long to come back."

"I knew you needed to get away. But if I could have told you how much better things got..."

"Did Dad stop drinking after the first stroke? Wade told me something about one years ago."

Sadie's eyes glistened with tears, but she smiled through them. "Oh, Kay, I wish you could have known him after he stopped. Between being sober and his painting—"

"Dad's the one who paints... painted?" Imagining her grease-stained, T-shirted father creating those beautiful portraits was beyond her.

"If you had known him before he went to war, you wouldn't have been surprised. His sensitive soul came back so wounded."

Kay shook her head slowly. Her mother had never talked so openly about her father.

"And I almost missed our golden years. I was going to leave him, you know. That's what caused the first stroke, I think. He came home while I was packing to go find you."

"But when I called and asked you to come live with me—"

"Your leaving had made me think long and hard. I talked to the chaplain here at the hospital, and he told me my first responsibility should have been to you. I shouldn't have let you grow up in a home with so much anger."

"You told the chaplain about it?"

"Had to. When you left I realized how bad things had gotten. So I decided I'd go find you, wherever you were."

A nurse entered to check Sadie's vital signs. Kay thought of the many times she had known she was interrupting an important conversation when she came into her patients' rooms. She had always hurried to finish and leave, but this nurse seemed to dawdle. When finally she left, Sadie had drifted off again. Kay wanted to jiggle her awake but knew the important role rest played in recovery.

She remembered the desperation that had made her call home. Her first ultrasound indicated twins. All her bravado and determination to raise her child alone collapsed at the thought of caring for two. She called her mother, hoping to convince her to leave her father and come live with her in Spokane. However, before Kay could tell her mother about the ultrasound, Sadie broke down and cried, sobbing between the words, "Your daddy needs me more than ever." Kay had slammed the phone down and never called again.

She filled the time waiting for her mother to awaken by praying and trying to come to grips with new images of her father. In a wheelchair in the aisle of a church. Lifting a paintbrush away from her portrait on the easel. Holding her mother's hand, moments before he died.

Kay dozed off in her chair and jumped when the nurse returned. The room had grown dark, and the nurse flipped on the lights. Kay's eyes squinted, not prepared for the brightness. Her mind felt no more ready to grasp what her mother had told her. She had to keep herself from tapping her foot, waiting for the nurse to finish changing the intravenous bag. When she finally left, Kay prompted her mother, "You were packing to come find me?"

Her mother seemed to struggle, confused. "I sent Wade to get you. I saw him and his father after the ambulance brought your dad and me in."

"No, Mama. Years ago. You were packing when Dad came in…"

Her mother's eyes focused far away. "Oh, yes." She shook her head. "He exploded. Never again saw his face go so red. So scared. He fell right down at my feet. I thought it was an act to get me to stay, but then the way his body slumped, I realized something was wrong. Just like this time. But this time the stroke hit when I was helping him into his wheelchair to go to the bathroom." Sadie wiped both her cheeks with her right hand; her left arm lay immobilized over her chest.

"I had come home from the hospital and was still in a state of shock when you called all those years ago. Otherwise, I would have told you what happened. Would have found out where you were. But it was for the best." She reached for Kay's hand. "Wasn't it?"

Kay considered her mother's question. Was it for the best? What would have happened if she had come home to help take care of her father? Seeing her pregnant, would Wade have stayed by her side? Or what if her mother had moved in with her to help her raise her twins? And if Sadie had left before Stu caught her packing, would he still have suffered the stroke? Or still be an angry drunk? But what ifs made no difference now. Her mother waited, looking to her for reassurance.

"I've had my share of blessings, Mama. Sounds like you have, too. I never would have thought Dad could be one of them."

Kay described nursing school and her work at Sacred Heart Hospital. She told Sadie about the condo she owned, and her friend Brenda's Jubilee plans. She talked her mother back to sleep, but never mentioned her twins, the most important blessings of her life.

CHAPTER 6

Franklin Hampton saw the look on his wife's face when he came home for dinner and knew to expect a dramatic evening. Wilhelmina's eyes shone, and she moved as if hearing her favorite song. This behavior always preceded a wild idea that would consume his wife's time and attention and inevitably cost him a fortune. But he wasn't alarmed. For too long now, Wilhelmina had been subdued and sad, worrying over their daughter-in-law Tiffany's health. It would be good for her to be swept up in a cause again.

He washed his hands and carried dishes to the table, listening to her hum. Franklin knew the routine. They'd ask each other about their days and exchange pleasantries. Sometime before he had finished his main course, however, she would give in to her excitement and expound about the next fundraiser or redecorating idea that had her mind in a whirl. He'd pretend concern and ask questions about feasibility and cost. She'd convince him with a rush of words about the merits of her idea, and before they turned out the lights that night, they would make amazing love, caught up in the adrenaline rush of a new adventure.

His steak was half finished and he had been savoring both its flavor and the anticipation in the room. She had only nibbled at her food. She set down her fork. Here it came. He braced himself good-naturedly.

"Franklin, I have an idea."

He leaned back in his chair, pleased with his intuition. He cocked an eyebrow and straightened his glasses. "How much will this one cost me?"

"A bundle. Both time and money, I'm afraid, but Franklin, I dearly want this."

How he loved his wife when she had that gleam in her eye. Other men might prefer a docile woman, but they'd never know the passion that his wife burned with, and enkindled in him. Even at their age, she still took care to look beautiful. His life with her never ran dull.

He crossed his arms. "Time and money. You'll work me ragged, woman."

"Franklin, I'd like you to look at some files." She seemed less sure of herself than she usually did at the beginning of a project. Something had her unshakeable confidence quivering.

When she returned to the table from the living room, she carried a number of manila folders. She sat and laid her hand on the top one. "I want us to adopt a child."

His heart nearly stopped. He caught his breath in spite of his courtroom training. He had prided himself in never showing surprise, but this, this—

She rushed on. "I know. We're not young. You're sixty-five and I'm... a bit younger..., but we wouldn't adopt a baby. These files hold the descriptions of some great candidates ranging in age from—"

"Wilhelmina! No!" He couldn't believe she was serious. They were planning their retirement. Wade would be taking over their law firm. They could go traveling like he had always dreamed.

"Franklin, please, hear me out." Her eyes looked so desperate that he lost his offensive advantage. He wanted to draw her into his arms and comfort her. But adoption, at their age?

"This first little girl, she's eight. Gertrude. Not a pretty name, but names can be changed, and she has the sweetest smile." She opened the file to show a photo of a cherub-faced child. Franklin remembered their Sharon at that age...

"Or if you'd prefer a boy, here's Darius. He looks a bit mischievous but we could handle that." She eased the second folder towards him, her eyes pleading.

"Wilhelmina, you can't possibly think—"

"Or here's Kamai and Jeremy. They're siblings and would love to be placed together. A four year old would keep us on our toes, but—"

"Willie, no. Stop." He closed all three files in one motion. "We're too old, Willie."

His beautiful, strong wife's chin trembled and he melted. He stood and drew her onto her feet and wrapped his arms around her. She rested her head on his shoulder and wept. He would do almost anything for this woman. He had gone against his better judgment more than once when she asked. But he could not return to parenting at his age. He knew she couldn't either.

"Wilhelmina, I love your soft heart and your fiery drive. You are a remarkable mother. You are going to be the perfect grandmother, too. Tiffany will get her heart. She and Wade are going be parents. You'll hold our grandchild in your arms, I know you will."

She stepped back from him and wiped her cheeks. She didn't meet his eyes, but murmured, "Do you really think so?"

"Absolutely. Tiffany is young. She's held out this long. Her turn must be coming soon."

"Franklin, these children need someone."

"You're right, Wilhelmina, but they deserve parents who can play with them, who'll still be young when they have children. Maybe we could look into some kind of foster grandparent program."

"I want our own, Franklin. But Tiffany is so sick. If Wade and Tiffany can't..."

He drew his wife back into his embrace. He didn't believe in a vindictive God, but the thought that maybe they carried some blame for the childless state of their son made his spine shudder from bottom to top.

"Tiffany will recover." He couldn't imagine losing their daughter-in-law. Their daughter's death had been devastating. To lose Tiffany, too, and with her their chance for grandchildren, that would be too much for any family.

"Maybe you're right." Her words were muffled against his shoulder. "We don't want Tiffany to think we've lost hope."

"She'll co-chair the next auction with you. You wait and see."

Wilhelmina disengaged herself and moved to the kitchen to bring dessert. The dance was gone from her walk.

Franklin racked his memory for some forgotten string he could pull to move Tiffany to the top of the list of people waiting for a heart.

#

Sadie Collie left the hospital, released into her daughter's care. Every bump or turn in the road jostled Sadie's shoulder and caused her to groan. By the end of the short drive to their home, Kay's nerves stood on edge and Sadie seemed exhausted. Kay helped her mother to the living room, where Sadie eased down onto the edge of the bed and melted into tears.

"Oh Mama, I'm sorry. There must be so many memories here of Dad. Do you want to sleep upstairs?"

"No! No, I'll feel closer to him down here. We've slept in this room together for near twenty years now." She nodded toward the easel. "Seems like he should be right over there, working on his portraits."

She reached out with her good arm and drew Kay to her side. "Oh Kay, your beautiful portrait. He'll never finish it now."

"It's all right, Mama. When I first saw it, I thought you were the artist, and I hoped you'd finish it, but now it seems right for it to stay the way it is. Things never were finished between us." Kay's voice broke and her eyes filled for what the relationship with her father should have been.

Her mother was a master at regaining control of her emotions. "Let's have a cup of tea like we used to when you volunteered at the hospital."

Kay nodded and moved to the kitchen. She realized why the swinging door was gone. It must have hampered her father's wheelchair movement around the house. Now conversation flowed between the two small rooms with only a slightly raised voice. "Who are the other people in the portraits, Mama?"

"People from all over the state. Portrait photographers send your daddy photos and he renders them in acrylic. He's got quite a clientele. Or he did."

Kay filled the kettle and lit the gas burner. "He was quite talented."

"He had only started working on your portrait recently. Inspired timing, after all these years."

Kay brought a tray with cups, tea, and honey, remembering her mother's sweet-tooth preferences.

"He certainly had you on his thoughts these last months. Often he'd make up stories about what you might be doing now. He figured you were married, had a couple children, lived in a little house... Why, what's the matter, dear? You look white as the wall."

Kay shook the coincidences out of her mind. "Nothing. Guess I'm thrown by how fast things can change." She hurried to stop the whistling of the teakettle, and with the twist of the burner control, she made up her mind. Certainly her mother deserved to know about her grandchildren. She could trust Sadie not to tell Wade. "Mama, Dad's guess wasn't far off—"

The sound of a knock at the back door cut Kay's words short.

"Oh, hello, Kay." Sensible-shoed Madge Pike was letting herself into the kitchen, followed by an older, smaller woman with an extended, wrinkly neck that reminded Kay of a turtle. "This is Agnes Swanson. Your mother ready for visitors?" She pushed past Kay and made her way into the living room.

"Nice to meet you, Kay." Agnes's head bobbed and her grin spread. "Sadie and Stu always said such nice things about you. You were quite a student, weren't you?"

Kay smiled in spite of the irritation she felt with Madge. "Nice to meet you, Agnes. You're part of the hospitality committee, too?" This woman with her ready cheerfulness fit the image much better.

"No, I'm head of the prayer shawl committee. Got one right here." She lifted a paper shopping bag, with handles adorned by a ribbon. "Time Sadie received one herself. May I?"

Kay nodded and Agnes slipped past her into the living room. Kay lifted two more cups and the teapot down from the cupboard, making a mental note as she filled the pot with the boiling water to lower the items her mother would need to reach. She followed their guests into the living room.

Sadie lifted what Kay would have guessed to be a dove-grey afghan from the paper bag. "Oh, Agnes, it's beautiful. Judging from these even stitches you made this one yourself, didn't you?" She leaned forward for a gentle side hug. "Thank you, dear."

"I figured it was high time you received one after the countless shawls you've donated. And your stitches are every bit as even as mine. I had a blue one from one of the new knitters, but bless her heart, you can tell what her mood was on every row she knits. Tight stitches on bad days, loose ones on the good. Judging from how many are tight, we should be keeping her in our prayers."

Kay ran her hand over the knitting and its softness tempted her to snuggle her face right into it. "This is heavenly. What exactly is a prayer shawl?"

Sadie's face shone with pride. "Several of the ladies of the church knit or crochet these while they pray for whoever will receive it. When we know of someone who's grieving..."

Her voice broke and Agnes continued, "Or who needs a reminder that he or she is loved, we bring it by and visit a spell."

Kay thought of the patients who didn't receive any company during their stay in her hospital and knew what a visit and such a gift would mean to them. "What a lovely idea."

Gruff Madge poured the tea that Kay had left steeping. "Sadie, I'm sure sorry about Stu. Church didn't seem right without his wheelchair in the aisle Sunday. I knew something was wrong when you two weren't there. Terrible thing, strokes."

"This one at least. The first one could have taken my Stu from me, but instead it gave me back the sweet Stu I first fell in love with. That stroke was a blessing."

"Hard to believe that gentle man was the same one who used to beat you."

Kay couldn't believe her ears. Didn't Madge know some things weren't said? And had her mother truly told these women about those times Kay had worked so hard to keep hidden?

"Mama?"

Sadie patted her hand. "It's all right, Kay. While your father was recuperating from his first stroke, I went to a program for families of alcoholics. They taught me that family secrets can allow horrible things to continue. The program sent me looking for my own support system, which I found at Our Savior." She smiled at her guests. "These dear friends welcomed me, took me under their wings, and held me up until I could stand on my own."

The four women sipped their tea in thoughtful silence for a moment, until Madge stood suddenly. "Can't stay. You need your rest, Sadie. Now swing those legs over and slip under the covers." She turned to Kay. "You take care of her, you hear?"

Agnes stood and handed Kay a business-sized card, embellished with lilacs. "Here's my phone number. You call if you need anything. I live only a few blocks away."

Kay rose to see them out.

Madge, who had already carried her cup to the kitchen sink, disappeared out the back door. Agnes followed but turned before closing the door. "Do call. We love your mama."

When Kay came back into the living room, her mother looked at her with a lopsided grin. "Madge is a bit protective. Now, what were you about to say before they came in?"

"Never mind, Mama. You need some rest. We'll have time to catch up later."

CHAPTER 7

The next Sunday, Kay entered the little church exhausted. Helping her mother get ready had proven quite an undertaking. Dress after dress hurt her too much when she struggled to get her arm into the sleeve. Finally, they had settled on a navy outfit that buttoned down the front. Sadie wouldn't consider going to church without nylons, so the two had wriggled together to pull them up. Luckily, Sadie found the whole undertaking funny. Kay felt her cheeks burn and didn't meet her mother's eyes. Dressing Sadie felt more awkward than helping her patients. And the struggle brought back emotions from the distant days when she used to help little Dana pull up her tights.

Kay paused at a back row, but Sadie continued up the aisle to the first pew. She rubbed her hand gently along the wooden arm and then took her seat. Kay hurried to catch up and join her mother. She had never sat in the front row of a church and would have preferred to be in the back where she could see without being seen. She hadn't taken much time to get herself ready. In fact, she tried to remember if she had brushed her own hair. But once the choir began to sing, she lost her self-consciousness and relaxed into the beautiful music. Maybe she would be able to rest during this time of worship.

The church appealed to her in its simplicity. Where she had imagined heavy gold and rich ornamentation, she saw instead simple, beautiful wood. Rather than stained glass, the windows were a translucent cloudy blue. The ceiling was also blue, and the effect focused her attention on things above.

Reverend Rob nodded in Sadie's direction and asked the congregation to offer a silent prayer in thanksgiving for their own "man on wheels" who had occupied the front of their aisle for so many years.

Then he suggested a show of support for "our dear Sadie," and Kay jumped at the thunderous applause. Sadie stood, turned to those behind her and blew them all a kiss.

"And welcome, Kay. We join your mother in being delighted to have you with us." Kay's cheeks warmed again, but she nodded her appreciation.

The scripture readings passed before Kay realized her mind had wandered. She felt like a child whose guilt might be obvious, and she kept her eyes downcast. But when the minister delivered his sermon, he held her captivated.

"How many of you feel overwhelmed by having too much to do?" He scanned his silent flock and grinned. "How many of you are so tired you don't have energy to raise your hands?"

This brought laughs and Kay could see hesitant waves off to her side. A mental image tickled her. She could picture a fisher of men casting his line out into the water.

"Anyone who would appreciate one extra day in their week, clap your hands." From the rustling and applause behind her, Kay realized many people shared her beleaguered experience. Exhaustion wasn't new to Kay. From the day she learned she was pregnant, less than a month after her marriage, her life had overwhelmed her. A matter of weeks ago she had wondered whether she could adjust to the slower pace as her nest emptied. She hadn't needed to worry. Looking at her mother out of the corner of her eye, she almost chuckled. Her life certainly hadn't slowed.

"What would you say if I told you God wants to nurture you, to give you the rest you can't find time for? That He wants to see you refreshed, having fun, truly enjoying life?"

Kay felt the minister was speaking directly to her. Was she nibbling at his bait?

"How do I know He wants this? Because He gave us the Sabbath."

The bubble of expectation he had built burst.

The minister must have felt it, too, because he leaned forward. "Let me ask you something else. How many feel there is more than we can possibly do, but we are the only ones who can do it?"

This time Kay turned her head and saw many hands. She even half raised her own.

"How many of us take pride in being able to handle what comes our way? We're pressured, but so far, we've managed."

A man in the front row on the other side of the aisle crossed his arms and smiled with satisfaction.

"So we're self-made men? …Or women? Self-reliant?"

Reverend Rob, master of timing, Kay thought.

"No wonder we are worn out. We're trying to be God." He paused and gazed around, letting his words sink in. "We've taken the day God gave us to rest and be refreshed, and we've pushed more and more work into it. But that isn't His plan. He intends to nurture us always, but particularly on one day each week. He offers us restoration, and we refuse the gift, saying we don't have time."

Kay listened, but shook her head. She figured he had never been a single parent. She had to keep herself from crossing her arms.

"I know what you're thinking. 'If that guy were in touch with the today's world he'd realize we already don't have enough time to get it all done. No way can we take one day off.' But what does God ask of us? To trust Him. To love Him. To spend time with Him. To show others His love through our actions."

The congregation was silent. Hooked? The minister tugged the line he held them on. "I know I've stood here time and again and exhorted you to live your lives for others. I've appealed to you to add to your busyness by volunteering, by ministering to others, by reaching out to the less fortunate. And you know yourselves that Jesus asked us to do those things. Feed His hungry, visit His sick, guide His little ones. I'm not asking you to stop that."

Kay relaxed her clenched hands a bit. She had spent her life taking care of two of God's little ones and not simply visiting His sick, but helping them heal. Her life was built on doing for others. She wouldn't believe anyone who said those choices were wrong.

"My friends, think of how good it feels when you bring food to a neighbor recently home from the hospital." He nodded toward Sadie and then looked out over his congregation. "Remember the glow you get at Christmas when you sponsor a needy family or donate a toy to a child? And yet many of us deny others that good feeling."

Kay imagined the minister reeling them back in.

"Aren't we a little selfish when we don't let people do things for us? That would be bad enough, but then when God wants us to take a day, His day, and refrain from work, we say 'no thanks.'"

Kay glanced at her mother, who was nodding her head. She imagined her mother caught in the minister's net. Her mother, who for years worked whatever day, whatever shift the hospital needed her. Like mother, like daughter. Nurses, especially new nurses, rarely could choose their workdays. And what would happen to patients with emergencies if doctors and nurses refused to work on Sundays?

But the minister was one cast ahead of her. "You might understandably ask me why I'm standing up here preaching, doing my work, on a Sunday. Or how police or fire fighters could refuse to help others on Sunday. Or for that matter, how a parent could skip diaper changes or meal preparation. Jesus understood such needs. He spoke of rescuing an ox from a pit on the Sabbath, and He himself healed an invalid on the holy day.

This time Kay nodded.

"But He also took time away to pray, trips to the mountains, or out to a garden. He knew how much we need our rest."

The minister rose up on his toes and leaned forward at the pulpit. Kay imagined his line reaching the middle of a stream. "My friends, I've challenged you before. I asked you to increase your charity offerings, your donations, to the point of discomfort. You responded bigheartedly and I suspect you learned God can't be outdone in generosity. When you sacrifice, He provides.

"I'm challenging you to sacrifice, not your money, but even more precious, your time. Give Him Sunday if you can, another day if you must, and rely on His generous provision to help you accomplish the truly necessary things. Trust Him. Spend your Sabbath day enjoying your family, visiting friends, renewing yourselves physically, mentally, emotionally, spiritually, or socially. Tell me—or better yet, witness to each other—the gifts He gives you when you give Him one day."

Reverend Rob smiled with tenderness at his catch, then took his seat. The choir began a song that was familiar to Kay from her own church. She would have to give this idea of a nurturing God some thought, but she doubted she would change how she used her Sundays. In Spokane, now that she had put in enough years to secure the dayshift on weekdays, she shopped for the week's groceries on Sundays. And though she always intended to do laundry on Saturday, she usually was folding the last load at bedtime on the Sabbath.

Her time with Brenda certainly was refreshing each Sunday morning. At least half her day was spent the way the minister suggested. But for now, too many things required attention at her mother's house. Bathroom walls needed a good scrubbing, maybe even a fresh coat of paint. Sadie had done an admirable job keeping the house fairly clean, but there were tasks a woman in her sixties shouldn't have to tackle alone. And oh, the garage…

#

Back in the little two-story house, Kay's mother wrapped herself in both the prayer shawl and her sorrow. Kay wished she could comfort her. Strange that the death of the man Kay had wanted to protect her mother from for years now caused her so much pain. That was all Kay had known of him, the hurt he caused. She had trouble imagining that between the pain he inflicted in her childhood and the grief so present on her mother's face today, he had brought joy. Kay regretted that she had never known the true Stuart Collie. As she looked around her, she also regretted that he had left so much undone. Not that he could help it, she reminded herself.

"Sit, Kay. It's Sunday."

"There's so much to do..."

"Please, let's talk a while." Sadie patted the bed next to her.

Kay rolled her shoulders and took the seat.

"Mama, could you tell me about the good years? Would that be too hard on you?"

Sadie grinned. "Oh, Kay, that'd give me comfort. You know, people seem to be afraid to talk about your father now, worried they'll make me sad. But it'd be worse not to be able to speak about him. I'd love to have you hear about the better times."

Sadie started with the days long ago when she first loved a boy, before he became a soldier and lost his way. Kay tried to imagine her father as the shy teenager who earned money for their dates by playing saxophone in a band.

She had never before heard about the baby Sadie miscarried before Kay. Kay had often imagined having a big brother to look out for her. Maybe she had one in heaven.

Sadie showed her some of the letters she had saved from Stu when he was in the Army. His handwriting was strong, but elegant. A hint of the artist he later would become.

Halfway through the stack of letters, the handwriting deteriorated and slanted across lines less regular. She could picture his hand shaking as she skimmed his words. "War has no winners, Sadie. We all lost something dear by being here. I know I'll never feel wholly human again. I find myself more angry than afraid. I don't know if I'll ever recover."

Kay set the page down and looked at her mother. "This is heartbreaking."

"He came back a different man. He couldn't overcome his anger for years. None of the years you knew him. But I knew my idealistic Stu hid in there somewhere. I think he drank to keep the inner Stu quiet. When he finally got sober after his stroke, he had to cry for days. He finally mourned his lost innocence."

"What transformed him? It had to be more than abstinence from alcohol."

"The counseling helped him forgive himself and forgive other people. But I think his soul began its healing when he started to create beautiful paintings." She raised her good arm toward the easel. "Bring me some of the portraits, would you?"

Kay released her own from the clamps and brought several others from the stack near the easel. Her mother moved Kay's to the bottom of the pile. "Look at the eyes." She shifted one portrait after another. Each face was stunning but Sadie was right, it was their eyes that captivated.

"Something shifted in your father when he began to paint people. Now, bring the envelope with the original photos in it."

Kay did, and Sadie matched the photos with the portraits. In each case, the portrait portrayed a different expression than the photo.

"The portrait people are wiser than the photo people." Wiser, was that the right word?

"Exactly. Somehow your father had found some peace with this life and was able to give a little of it to each of his subjects."

Sadie placed Kay's portrait on top. She pointed to Kay's senior photo on the wall. "In your photo you are smiling, but with caution. You had to stay on guard in this house. When I look at you now, I see a strong, capable young woman, determined to prove herself to an unfair world. I hope someday you'll find the peace and wisdom your father painted for you."

Kay studied the portrait and squinted to envision what her mother saw. Earlier she had seen caution and hope. Her mother perceived serenity and wisdom. Kay considered herself in the mirror on the wall. She hoped her patients found compassion in her face. Maybe someday, if she ever found peace, she would recognize it in the painting.

#

Kay felt out of her element later that week at her father's memorial service. She sat in the front row again with her mother, who appeared pale but serene. A table that held the mahogany urn stood at the same place in the aisle where her father's wheelchair had parked, she was told, every Sunday for years. Kay wished she could sit farther from the container that held her father's ashes.

Her mother had been pleased to learn Kay, too, had found solace and support in a worship community. Kay didn't share with Sadie that her son's early teen years drove her to church. Yet, she understood the refuge her mother found from the struggles of daily life. Perhaps Kay could share some of that safe harbor in her mother's church.

As the service progressed, many people spoke about the gentle man with the good-natured humor whose patient endurance of his disability was an example to them in times of trouble. Kay couldn't relate to their memories of him, but she felt loved and upheld by the final hymn and the surprising number of mourners who filed past the urn to say a prayer, then stopped to whisper their sympathies to her mother and her.

A familiar voice captured Kay's attention.

"I'm sorry for your loss, Mrs. Collie." Wade, with a face as haggard as if he had lost his own father, stood with her mother's hand in his. After Sadie thanked him and lifted onto tiptoes to kiss his cheek, he moved in front of Kay.

"Kathleen, I am so very sorry." He was the only one besides her mother who had ever called her by her full name, and Sadie only used Kathleen in reprimand. Wade saved it for especially tender moments. The last time she heard it was during his wedding vows.

His eyes grew as moist as hers felt. He gave her a stiff hug, which she was slow to release. She realized their awkward moment was holding up the line and drawing attention. She stepped back. He moved on.

To Kay's chagrin, Madge followed next in line. She embraced Sadie gently but only offered a perfunctory nod in Kay's direction. The woman was a constant accusation to Kay. Her mother noticed the slight and patted Kay's hand.

She wondered what exactly Wade was sorry about. Her father's death? Or did his words carry meaning from the past, an apology for abandoning her? She shook her head for embracing hopes she should have released when he signed their short marriage away.

CHAPTER 8

The next few days felt much like the long, tiring days of her twins' preschool years. Her care for her mother and the house, compounded by managing her Spokane life from a distance, left her exhausted each night. Folding clothes or helping her mother with gentle stretches, her thoughts frequently returned to Wade. With strict discipline forged through the years, she reminded herself he was married. Her time with him was over. She even managed a prayer for Tiffany's health.

Before her mother's discharge, she had bought some inexpensive clothes and a cell phone, but she had been afraid to leave Sadie alone once she came home. When her mother's many friends visited and offered help, she might hurry to get groceries but otherwise Kay assured them she and her mother could manage fine.

Kay kept going by telling herself how admirably her mother seemed to be adjusting to widowhood. Physically Sadie seemed weak and struggled to stay ahead of her pain, but Kay didn't question the resilience of her mother's spirit. Sadie had managed her life without the help of a husband throughout Kay's childhood. She had never depended on her husband financially, like many widows, but rather had always supported herself. No doubt, she would return to her work at the hospital once she healed. Kay winced at the thought of Sadie scrubbing with a partially recovered shoulder. Would the hospital's retirement pay keep Sadie comfortable when that time came?

As for missing her father, Kay knew her mother had lived for years without his true participation in her life. She could do so again. Sadie would soon move past the crying Kay heard each night after she had gone upstairs to her room. The first night she had hurried to her mother to offer more pain medication, but Sadie sent her back upstairs with a wave of her hand. "Drugs won't help the pain in my heart, dear." After that night, Kay simply lay in her bed listening, reliving her own heartbreak and midnight tears.

She had fully intended to whip the house, yard, and even garage into shape, but caring for her mother had taken more hours and energy than she expected. By the time they had cringed through the physical therapy exercises, struggled her into clothes, and eaten breakfast, it seemed the day was half over. Between grocery shopping, meals, laundry, and hosting the numerous people who dropped by, she managed little more than the essentials.

If that weren't enough, on Friday the snow began. Kay had been happy to leave the Montana winters behind. Though Spokane suffered its share of winter, in Butte snow frequently started as early as September and lasted easily into April. She recalled one Fourth of July when tiny ice crystals drifted down during the parade.

Now outside her bedroom window, large snowflakes fell fast and heavy in the cone of visibility below the streetlight. If this kept up there would be quite an accumulation before morning. She groaned. She could add shoveling sidewalks to her list of duties. If only she had made room in the garage for the car. Now she would need to sweep it off and probably have to shovel the driveway, too. So much for a workless Sunday. It would take both Saturday and all day Sunday to accomplish what needed to be done.

In the morning, Kay woke to the bluish light that reflected into her room from the snow below. Unlike the days when it lifted her heart to know her whole world wore a mantle of white, this morning it felt like one more burden than she could handle. She wished her mother had money enough to replace the old storm windows; she had forgotten how cold her room could be. Kay lifted the curtain aside and looked out over the city. A fresh snowfall was the only time that Butte seemed beautiful to her. Skeletal mine frames, aging cars, and even the gaping rim of the Berkeley Pit wore a new polar bear coat.

Her eyes focused closer and her jaw clenched. No wonder she was so cold. The storm windows hadn't been hung yet. She remembered balancing on the rickety ladder each year while her mother held it from below. They always tried to hurry through the task when her father wasn't home. The thought of him climbing the ladder in his unsteady state frightened Kay more than doing it herself. The last thing they could afford was for him to wind up in the hospital. She smiled at the thought now. Ending up in the hospital was what had finally sobered him and changed his life.

When she realized she would need to climb the ladder again, this time in snow, all humor deserted her. She bowed her head, "God, I'm struggling to do everything I can here. The minister says we need to trust You to help us accomplish what we must, and show our trust by taking Your day off. Forgive me, I don't see any way I can manage that."

She hurried out of her pajamas and into her clothes, shivering all the while. She left the upstairs and tiptoed past her mother's bed in the living room, hoping to get something warm made for them for breakfast before Sadie woke.

"Rice pudding day!" her mother whispered excitedly before Kay made it to the kitchen. "Do you remember?"

Kay hadn't remembered, but her mother's words brought a rumble to her stomach. As a child, Kay and her mother had always celebrated the first snow by making rice pudding. Her mother said it was her family's tradition.

"Coming right up!" With the microwave, she could have warm rice pudding ready in about twenty minutes. Though it had always been a rare dessert as a child, who said it couldn't be a warm breakfast?

Kay's mother threw off the blankets with her good arm and struggled into a sitting position. As she slid her feet into her slippers, she called, "I'll help!"

The roles reversed from Kay's childhood but the spontaneous fun bubbled again.

As they savored the last spoonful from their bowls, Kay and Sadie heard a motor start up near the house. Kay opened the living room drapes, revealing the white blanketed yard. A pickup truck rumbled up and parked behind another one. Two young men joined a third who was making quick work of clearing Sadie's sidewalk with his powered snow blower.

Sadie joined Kay at the window. "Bless those boys. It's one of the youth service groups from church."

The three carried on a loud conversation over the sound of the blower but Kay couldn't make out their words. One glanced at the window and waved. Kay and Sadie returned the greeting as he approached the house.

Kay opened the door.

"Hi, Miss Collie. I'm Daniel Davis. We're your work crew for a day. You and Miss Sadie start making a list and we'll come get our orders as soon as we have your sidewalks done and your driveway cleared off."

Kay stood dumbfounded, but Sadie leaned around her. "Wonderful! Thank you, Daniel. We'll get hot chocolate going, too."

Within hours they had hung storm windows, stacked or hauled away the garage clutter, insulated outdoor vents and faucets, and covered the rose bush. Indoors, a pipe no longer leaked, and bathroom walls shone. The young men feasted on rice pudding and hot chocolate, then waved goodbye as they moved on to help another of the church's elderly.

Kay closed the door and Sadie stood with one hand on her hip. "You see, Kay Collie? God's going to provide for us. He always has."

"They've come before?"

"These or others. I think God delights in surprising us with His providence in ways like this. I couldn't count the times He's come through when I needed Him most. He's how we survived all those years before the stroke."

Kay shook her head slowly. Her little family, too, had made it through her children's growing years when time after time she wasn't sure how they would. She had stood taller and worked harder. At the time, she had thought she made her own success. Now, she wondered how much of their survival God had arranged.

Once when she grew frantic with trying to survive on the little sleep a mother of two infants snatches, an eleven year old from a nearby condo asked if she could come learn about babies to become a good babysitter. She had returned many days after school and one more pair of hands had been invaluable.

And the dayshift nurse who happened to be looking for someone to trade childcare right when Kay needed to return from maternity leave to working afternoon shift, was she God's help? Once Dana had needed her tonsils removed. To pay the deductible from her tight budget, Kay had foregone buying Christmas presents. Christmas Eve, a hospital charity knocked on her door and brought in two boxes of food and one of toys. She remembered her shame at the time, but if she had seen the charity as an example of God's delight in providing, the way her mother did...

The next day after church, Kay and her mother relaxed and exchanged stories from their time apart. Kay dabbled a bit with her father's paints and wondered when she last had time to play. She tried to learn how to knit, but her mother, having only one good hand, wasn't able to demonstrate. They gave up, but not before they were both "in stitches."

That afternoon Kay felt more rested and refreshed than she had in a long time. But in bed that night, her worries returned. How would she pay for Dana's college without overtime? Should she tell her mother about the twins? Would Wade ever forgive her for keeping them from him if he found out? Would the twins?

#

By the fourth Sunday of her stay in Montana, Kay thought she might actually get through this all. In another couple of weeks, her mother should be independent. Maybe no secrets would need to be revealed. She had told her children she'd been assigned to work as a private nurse for a short time. She gave them her new cell phone number, and they called each Sunday afternoon to tell her about their week.

She listened that Sunday afternoon, as always, with the door to her room closed. Dana was adjusting to college in Seattle. She liked her roommate and together they made many friends from classes and the dorm. Chemistry proved harder than in high school, but she had learned determination from her mother. She was looking forward to coming home for the Columbus Day three-day weekend.

If all went as hoped with Sadie's recovery, Kay figured she would be back in Spokane by then. She said goodbye, missing her daughter, yet relieved the distance between them meant she didn't have more to explain.

But then Drew's call came.

"Mom, I have my new orders. I'll train for six months in Georgia, and then be assigned overseas."

Her heart jolted. "Overseas?" The computer components that Drew had tinkered with cluttered his room during his high school years and reminded Kay of the old cars that had littered her father's yard, waiting for him to be thirsty enough to fix them and return them to their owners. Unlike her dad, however, Drew's puttering enhanced his future. He had tested so high in his entrance exams that the Army had assigned him to computer training. Kay had hoped that would keep him state-side.

"Mom, it could be the Middle East. You know what can happen there."

He paused and Kay closed her eyes against the future.

"Don't get upset, Mom, but before I go, I want to know about my dad."

"We've been through this before. I don't want—"

"I don't want to die not knowing who I am." His voice was steady, determined.

Kay stalled. It was a demand that she knew would come someday. The twins had a right to know. Though her fear of losing custody of her children still gripped her, that danger had past. They were adults now and no longer subject to the whims of a custody court. However, she still could lose their hearts.

"Mom?"

"I need time, Drew. Do you have leave before Georgia?"

"I get a week, starting Columbus Day weekend."

She exhaled deeply. "Fly into Butte, Montana. I'll be ready to tell you everything then."

Less than two weeks. He was right. Truth was overdue. She called Dana back and told her about her brother's transfer and request. They agreed Dana, too, would fly to Butte for Columbus Day. The ironic timing struck Kay. Her children would embark like Columbus to explore a whole new world, a world of family. She imagined herself left behind on the shore.

Kay left her bedroom, feeling like a child who needed to confess to her mother some serious transgression.

Sadie rocked in one of the blue chairs, staring out the window.

"Mama, I need to talk to you."

Sadie turned toward Kay and nodded. "About time. You know these walls are paper thin."

Kay inhaled sharply at the memory of the blows she could hear land in her parents' bedroom. A nerve wave shivered up her spine. "You know, then?"

"I know you get two calls on Sundays. You greet them both, 'Hello, dear,' and you tell them both you love them before you say goodbye. Now unless you are keeping two men on the string, I'd say you have family that it's long past time to introduce."

Kay sat next to her mother. She ran her hand over the knitting that waited between the chairs. Its softness somehow added to her melancholy.

"You would have knitted baby blankets if you'd known."

CHAPTER 9

The conversation with her mother stretched into the night, punctuated with tears and hugs. In the morning, they both rose later than usual and needed to hurry to get Sadie to her physical therapy appointment in time. With an hour available, Kay squared her shoulders and forced herself to drive to the sturdy brick Hampton law offices. Wade hadn't wanted to follow his father's and his grandfather's footsteps after high school, but his parents had won that battle, too, obviously.

Vivid red lipstick framed the middle-aged receptionist's smile. She offered Kay a seat while she went to see if "Mr. Wade" was available. He followed the woman back out of his office and invited Kay in. She took a seat on the near side of his beautiful cherry desk.

"May I get you some coffee or tea?" His voice broke and he coughed to cleared it.

When she shook her head, he closed the door and sat on the far side of the desk, which now felt to Kay like an unbridgeable chasm.

"Wade, I need to talk to you. Could you sit over here with me?"

He conceded, taking a chair next to hers, and looked at her carefully. He reached as if to take her left hand, but seeing it, he pulled back and the concern in his eyes changed to coolness. "What's wrong? Is it your mom?"

"Wade, I've hidden something from you for all these years."

"Yes, yourself." The bitter tone to his answer tightened something inside her chest.

"You signed our marriage away!" she countered.

"You took $20,000 and left. My mother was right; money was all you wanted. That's why you married me!" He stood. "You broke my heart, Kay."

The tightness turned to throbbing. "What about my heart? You let them erase our marriage." He had no right to be angry. She stood. "This was a bad idea."

"Marrying you was the bad idea! I waited for you. I waited for years for you to come back."

She pushed a hand against her sternum to hold back her battering-ram heart. "You mustn't have searched too hard for me! I didn't change my name. I was only 300 miles away, at Gonzaga, one of the schools that accepted me. It wasn't that difficult."

This wasn't going to work. It still hurt too badly. The pounding in her chest reverberated in her head. She escaped out the door before she had time to break down completely.

She wrestled with her car door and slammed it behind her, trying to stifle her sobs. She watched the door to Wade's office and saw another door, another time. Nineteen years ago she had fled his dying sister's room, and then waited outside the hospital, sure that he would catch up with her and make it all right. He hadn't. He stayed with his parents and let them refuse to accept his new bride.

While Kay remembered, Wade emerged from the law office, glancing up and down the street, looking for her! Her heart lifted and she unlatched the car door handle. But something inside his office caught his attention before he let go of the door. No! He glanced once more down the street, turned, and disappeared inside.

He hadn't changed. He didn't deserve to know his children.

Like nineteen years ago, she was left no option but to retreat to her mother.

#

When Kay stormed out of his office, Wade decided not to allow her to run from him again.

As he strode past Mary's receptionist desk, she moved the phone away from her ear. "Mr. Wade, wait!"

"Later, Mary!" He held the door as he scanned the street, hoping to see Kay hurrying into her car. He had opened his mouth to call her name when he heard one word of Mary's frantic appeal.

"Hospital!"

He stopped abruptly and his anger collapsed. What was he doing? He groaned, caught between shoulds. Kay would drive away. His mistakes with Kay had made him vow he would be steadfast in his love for Tiffany. He had sworn he would never again let anything come between him and a wife. Not his wife's rejection of him. Not her failing heart. Not even his first love, Kay herself.

He resolutely turned back. Mary was holding the phone receiver out to him, her eyes wide with foreboding. "They said it's critical."

He thanked God for helping him turn back and took the phone.

"Mr. Hampton, you'd better come. Tiffany's condition is deteriorating. I'm sorry."

Every muscle in his body clenched. "Mary, tell my father I'll be at the hospital. It looks bad. Call Tiffany's parents." Mary nodded and Wade knew her tears were sincere. He toughened himself for what lay ahead and ran to his car.

When he arrived at the hospital, his lungs felt like they ignored his need for more air. He stopped to inhale and forced himself to calm down. Tiffany had been moved to ICU. When he found her, the doctor was removing his stethoscope from his ears. He drew Wade back out of the room and murmured his apologies. "We've run out of time. Her heart is giving up and there isn't a donor available."

Wade went to his wife's side and held her hand. She grasped his weakly. "I'm not going to make it."

He couldn't find words or trust his voice to answer, but kissed away tears on her cheeks.

She went on, catching her breath after each phrase. "I'm sorry, Wade. You were a good husband. Gave me all the love you could. I shouldn't have turned away..."

"You were dealing with too much."

"This heart. Our baby. So unfair. I took it out on you."

"I love you, Tiffany." He truly did. The kind of love that is a daily decision. Steadfast love.

"I know. You've always been here for me. You deserve to be happy, Wade."

Her hand relaxed and she sank deeper into the pillow, her gasps slowing but audible. He hadn't been able to say goodbye to his sister before she died, or Kay before she disappeared. Thank God for this chance with Tiffany. It wouldn't be long now before she, too, would leave him.

#

Kay helped her mother into the car. The older woman seemed worn from the efforts of her physical therapy. Kay was grateful to distract herself with her mother's needs. She turned the car toward their home.

"How did it go?" Kay asked.

"Not good. Hurts when they make me reach. They aren't happy with my slow progress." She turned her head away from Kay, but not before Kay had noted the flush of her cheeks.

"You'll get there, Mama. People heal at different rates, that's all." The words struck her as hollow. How long had she waited to heal from her broken marriage? She still waited. Sometimes healing didn't come. The thought of her mother's pain brought a return of the tears she had carefully washed away in a McDonald's restroom after leaving Wade's office. She sniffed and her mother turned quickly to face her.

"What is it, dear? Here I am, an old fool feeling sorry for myself. Did you talk to Wade?"

Kay stopped at a red light, mindful of the icy street. She remembered how easily her children could talk to her while she drove in the car. Something about the lack of eye contact made difficult conversations less troublesome, she guessed.

"We didn't get far before I stormed out. I didn't realize he was so angry with me."

"You left him. You should have fought for him." These were the first words of rebuke her mother had uttered since Kay's return.

"You're mad, too. You blame me for leaving, just like he does."

"Wade had buried his sister and his heart ached for his parents, I'm sure. He needed time to realize his actions might mean he would lose you, too. You didn't give him time to see his mistake."

"I didn't have time. I didn't know when I'd start to show. Wilhelmina would have taken my babies, like she took him."

"And you were terrified of your father."

"Dad might have killed me if he knew. He hated Wade."

Out of the corner of her eye, Kay noticed her mother flinch and she regretted her tone.

Sadie's exhale sounded controlled. "Why Spokane?"

"Right before Mrs. Hampton came to me with those awful papers, Gonzaga's financial aid offer arrived in the mail. It was almost a full-ride scholarship. I hadn't told anyone about applying to them. Seemed like such a financial reach, I didn't think there was much chance of being able to go."

Realization struck with such force that Kay couldn't continue to drive. She pulled over to park, her wheels needing to escape the snow ruts to approach the curb. She hadn't told anyone about Gonzaga. Not even Wade? A distinct possibility.

"Oh, Mama, he didn't know to look there."

"Neither did I." The sadness in her mother's voice renewed Kay's guilt.

"I'm so sorry, Mama."

Sadie took her time before responding. "Love always requires sacrifice but maybe sometimes we must break a promise—hoping the one we love will understand and forgive—to protect the most vulnerable."

Kay waited for an explanation.

Her mother's face grew more serious. "Wade broke his promise to you for his parents' sake. Maybe I should have broken one, too. I was good at the sacrifice love requires, but your father wasn't. I thought I needed to stay with him no matter what because of my wedding vows. Now I know staying with him was a promise I should have broken for your sake, and my own. When you have a child, you make an unspoken vow to love and protect her. I should have protected us both from him."

"But then the stroke."

"The stroke gave him time in the hospital to sober up. But he decided to quit drinking on his own. I think realizing I would leave him was what did it. If I wanted to torture myself, I'd wonder if I could have stood up to him years earlier and he would have stopped. I could have maybe prevented his strokes. I definitely might have kept you from leaving. And I would have held my grandbabies."

The sorrow on her mother's face went straight to Kay's heart. "I love you, Mama. You'll meet the twins soon. We'll start over."

Her mother reached awkwardly to pat her with her good right hand. "That's all we can ever do. Start from where we are."

"Our best wasn't great, but I guess it was all we had."

"I know you might not understand this, but maybe Wade and your daddy did the best they could, too."

"You're right, Mama. That's more than I can believe." She shifted out of park, turned back toward the lane, and allowed her wheels to find the ruts worn slippery by other cars.

When she drove into the garage at home, her mother hesitated before getting out. "You still need to tell Wade before the twins get here."

Kay nodded, knowing that her two worlds neared the end of their fated trajectories. Collision was inevitable and always had been.

CHAPTER 10

Less than a week later, Madge knocked only long enough on the back door to announce her entrance into the kitchen. "I came early, so you'd have time to get ready."

"For what?" Kay scanned her memory for some forgotten commitment, but she had so little life outside the house that it didn't take long.

"For Tiffany's funeral. I know you and Wade were close once. Figured you'd want to go. I'll stay with your mom until you're back."

Kay dropped into a kitchen chair. "She died? She was waiting for a heart."

"Didn't come in time. Thought you would have known." Madge looked down at the floor and pushed away a dust bunny with her toe. "I'm sorry I didn't break the news better. Funeral's at nine-thirty at the Episcopal church."

Kay didn't want this woman's help. She could manage on her own. But Wade must be heart-broken. And he had come to her father's funeral. She glanced at the clock and hurried out of the kitchen. "Thank you, Madge. I won't stay long."

"Stay as long as you need. Your mother and I haven't been able to get in a good visit with you around."

#

Kay paused inside the door of the large church. The slight scent of incense flooded her mind and heart with memories. The last time she had been in this building was for Sharon Hampton's funeral. The final time she saw Wade before she left. She remembered the roller coaster of emotions that led to that day.

The pride of graduation day. The joyful abandon of riding home with Wade. Her fear when she realized they had forgotten to drop her off a block away. The fear rising to terror when she stepped into the living room and realized her father had seen her get out of the car. That blasted old Mustang. Simply based on the model, her father hated Wade. It was the car of his dreams and now some "stupid kid, wet behind the ears" drove his daughter home in it. He could keep the car, her father said, but he'd never have his daughter.

The pain of her father's beating enkindled enough defiance to escape while he drained the last of a bottle. She ran all the way from her poor neighborhood to Wade's beautiful home....

Kay chose a seat near the back of the church and closed her eyes. She could feel the memories tensing her muscles, and a slight shiver spread outward from her spine and caused her hands to shake.

She worked to calm herself, inhaled some deep, slow breaths, and held on to the sweeter memories of those days: Wade answering the door and wrapping her in his protective embrace. Him grabbing a change of clothes for himself and some of his sister's things for her, and then his car keys. The impulsive drive to Idaho where he rented a motel room and simply held her until she felt safe enough to fall asleep. The next morning when the justice of the peace considered her bruised face suspiciously, but then Wade's class ring sliding over her left ring finger and making it all worthwhile. Returning to the motel, where the completeness of Wade's love warmed her and sheltered her from her father's rage. She had found a man to treat her with the love and respect she'd never seen her father show her mother.

However, now years later in the church, Kay couldn't hold on to the beauty and security of that love. Her thoughts broke through her defenses, and her short-lived calm surrendered to pain. They had returned to Butte scared, yet determined to share their news with their families. Then Wade's family wasn't home. Instead, a note waited for Wade begging him to hurry to the hospital. His sixteen-year-old sister had been in a car accident. The note was written about the same time they had been exchanging their vows, for better, for worse.

They had hurried to the hospital but his parents, already distraught, took one look at Kay wearing his sister's dress and with their reaction, her future shifted. She ran outside and when Wade didn't follow her, fled to the only place left, her home, where luckily her father's drinking binge had kept him from missing her.

She blamed it on grief when Wade didn't call over several weeks as his sister's condition deteriorated. When Sharon Hampton died, it took all Kay's courage to attend the funeral. By then she had confirmed her suspicion, but hadn't had a chance to tell Wade she was pregnant. Clutching her hope that the news would save their marriage, she attended the service. She didn't sit in the front row with her husband and his family, but rather at the back of the church. Perhaps in this same pew.

Kay's fingers unconsciously moved to spin the simple band she had bought to replace Wade's class ring. In the months after their wedding and the years since, it protected her from unwanted questions. She had removed it, however, before leaving Spokane, and her finger still felt undressed.

Now their children were young adults, and she still hadn't told Wade about the twins. They had only exchanged enough words at his sister's funeral to agree to meet later that day at the hospital cafeteria during her candy striper break. Instead, his mother appeared brandishing annulment papers with Wade's signature. She offered $10,000 if Kay would sign and never contact him again.

Stunned to see his signature declaring their marriage void by reason of emotional duress, and shaken by the responsibility for the life their love had created, she wavered. A salty drop rolled down her cheeks and landed on his scrawled name. She brushed it away, and smeared the ink. If she were left to support this child alone, she would need all the financial help she could get.

"I won't sign that. I stand by my promises. But for $20,000 I'll sign something swearing to leave and never contact Wade again." She held out hope that he would find her and make things right.

Wilhelmina Hampton conceded, delighted, Kay supposed, to be rid of the girl she believed to be a gold digger. She never knew she had paid to ensure a life without grandchildren. Kay fled town that same day, afraid if she saw Wade she would never have the strength to leave. An influential woman in a family of lawyers who could take away her marriage might find a way to take her child, and Kay had to make sure she wouldn't get the chance.

Reverberations of the organ rumbled Kay out of her memories. She glanced around to see the church had filled. The casket and the family processed past her: an unfamiliar couple who must have been Tiffany's parents, followed by Wade and his parents. His mother scanned the crowd and met Kay's gaze. Her lips pursed, and Kay felt her own jaw clench. She had come in support of a past love and had no need to please his mother. Kay had kept her part of the agreement. And Wilhelmina had kept her son.

#

At the reception in the church hall following the service, Kay was grateful to be hailed to a table by Francie.

"Oh, Kay, I'm glad you made it. I wondered if you'd heard. But I guess the whole town knew, what with Wade's family being so prominent. How are you and your mom doing?"

"We're all right. I'm exhausted, though." Kay settled into the chair next to her friend. "Makes me realize what Mom's been going through for years taking care of my dad alone." Francie was one person she didn't feel she had to defend herself to.

"Yeah, my dad was sick for a long time. Liver trouble. Mom put up with a lot."

Kay nodded and knew from the look on Francie's face that her mother wasn't the only one. "Do you think they made the right choice, Francie? Our mothers? Was it right to stay with their husbands? They certainly hung on through the worst extremes of their wedding vows."

"I don't know, Kay. I hope I'd get out, especially for my kids' sake." She held Kay's gaze, then lowered her eyes. "Actually, that's what my husband did."

Kay waited, surprised.

"I caused a car accident four years ago. I was the drunk driver. Worse, I had my two daughters with me. Because I drove drunk and endangered the children, they sent me to prison for two years. The best and the worst thing that ever happened to me."

"What did your husband—"

"Allen."

"What did Allen do?"

"He took the girls and moved to Anaconda so his sister could help him with our daughters. In the first several weeks he visited, but neither of us knew what to say. I had no excuses or explanations. I didn't deserve his forgiveness, so I didn't ask for it. Then he stopped coming or writing. When I got out of prison, he said they didn't want to see me. I guess he didn't break his vow. We're still married, but he made sure the girls are safe."

"And you haven't seen them in all this time?"

"More accurate to say they haven't seen me. I park once and a while and watch them walk home from school."

Kay could feel her own eyes burn as Francie's filled.

Francie took a photo out of her purse. "After living as a Winters before I was married, I wanted some summer in their names. Rose is fourteen now and Daisy is seven."

"They're beautiful and look so sweet. It must kill you to be apart from them."

"I've been sober since the day of the accident, four years now. But I don't trust myself not to slip back. I can't risk hurting my girls."

Francie nodded toward Wade. "But you do have to admire steadfast love. Look at Wade, for instance." She lowered her voice. "Folks say as soon as Tiffany learned she had heart problems she locked him out of her life, if you know what I mean. But he never wavered from his vows. He stood by her right through to the end. I wonder how a guy becomes that faithful."

"Maybe he learns from his mistakes." As soon as the words were out, Kay wished she hadn't said them, but Francie nodded with a sympathetic smile. Did she know about their elopement and annulment? Kay realized such secrets were rarely harbored successfully in small towns, but with everyone focused on his sister's accident and with the influence their family held, it was possible.

Kay's mother had known. She had comforted Kay through the weeks afterwards, but Kay doubted she would have divulged her daughter's rejection, even though it seemed Sadie had since learned to keep secrets from ruling her own life.

Kay reached for her purse, the urge to show Francie the photos of her own children overcoming her careful vigilance.

A grating voice interrupted her moment of weakness. "Kay Collie, what convenient timing. Returning to town after all these years. Precisely in time for my daughter-in-law's funeral. Do I need to get out my checkbook again?" The words slurred together and the possibility of Wilhelmina Hampton being anything less than proper in public surprised Kay more than the venom behind them.

Kay slid her wallet back into her purse and stood. "I need to be going. Bye, Francie." She nodded at Wade's mother. "Mrs. Hampton, I'm sorry for your loss." She turned at the door for a last look and saw Wade hurrying toward her. Not wanting to make more of a scene, she slipped out and waited for him.

#

Franklin Hampton observed his son hastening toward the door. He glimpsed a woman leaving who disconcertingly resembled Kay Collie. The family had narrowly averted all the trouble that girl caused so many years ago. He noted Wade's determined stride and the way Wilhelmina blocked his path. Judging from their body language, he had better calm his wife. As he approached them, he heard the anger in her hissing voice.

"Don't you dare follow that woman. She had no right to be here!"

Her attempt at a whisper seemed to be drawing more attention than she realized.

Wade didn't answer but he didn't follow, either.

Franklin wrapped an arm around his son's back. "This is a hard day for all of us. We loved Tiffany. Your mother—"

"She's here to steal you again, Wade. You mark my words." In jabbing her finger at Wade, Wilhelmina spilled wine from the glass she clutched.

"Wilhelmina, dear, please." Franklin said.

Wade explained but with no patience in his voice, "Kay's in town for her mother. Mr. Collie died recently. Mrs. Collie had surgery and needed her help. Her being in Butte has nothing to do with me."

Franklin noted that Wade didn't tell her he was the one who delivered her mother's plea for Kay to return. Given the state of Wilhelmina's nerves, he counted it a wise choice.

"But here she is, at your wife's funeral. Unbelievable." Wilhelmina's back stiffened when Franklin put his arm around her to guide her away from the conversation, but she did walk with him to be seated at a table. "I am going to miss our Tiffany so much." She set her drink down and Franklin was moved by the sincere sorrow in her face. "She was the perfect daughter-in-law."

Franklin nodded and waited for the inevitable to follow.

"If only she could have had children."

Franklin exhaled with relief that Wade had moved to the buffet table. No need for him to hear this from his mother yet again. He slid the glass of wine discreetly away from his wife. "We'll all miss her. Terrible tragedy to go so young." He saw Wade fill a plate and hoped, yes, he was bringing it to Wilhelmina.

"Mother, would you like a little something?"

"Thank you, dear, yes. I'm feeling a bit light-headed."

Franklin warned Wade with a look. The last thing Wilhelmina needed was to see her son roll his eyes. The warning stopped the expression, but Wade sat and restarted the conversation where it had left off.

"I attended Kay's father's funeral. She came to return the gesture. I'm sure she didn't mean any disrespect."

"You should have warned me she was in town. Quite a shock, you know."

Franklin studied his son. He looked ghastly. Of course, he was burying his wife today after years of her poor health. These last months would have been enough to wear anyone down. Judging from the unsettled expression on Wade's face, Wilhelmina wasn't the only one adjusting to the idea of Kay Collie's return. Unfortunate timing.

His gaze moved to the door that had closed behind Kay Collie. He wondered again, as he had so many times before, had they done the right thing years ago? Might his son have found more happiness if they hadn't interfered? He cringed at the scowl his wife wore and knew his own home would have been less pleasant.

If only he could turn back the clock to his son's high school graduation. His wife had never been an easy woman, but before that day, she never needed the consolation of alcohol. Before the events that began that night, he had been proud of his own integrity.

CHAPTER 11

When Wade didn't follow her outside the church hall, Kay shook her head and returned to her car. Back at Sadie's house, Madge stood to leave as soon as Kay came in. Kay delayed her with a hand on her sleeve. "Thank you, Madge. I appreciate your thoughtfulness."

Madge nodded and hurried out the back door.

"Honestly, Mama, that woman amazes me. She's so gruff, but hides a soft heart, too."

"People aren't all good or all bad, my Katie girl. You've got to focus on their good side to appreciate them."

"Is that what you did with Dad?"

Her mother laughed. "There were times I had to squint real hard to focus."

A memory of her mother with an eye swollen shut made her stomach jolt.

"People make horrible mistakes, Kay. Wade did. His mother did. God knows, I did. But we learn from them and move on. Let go of your anger. You've a right to it, but it's not doing you any good."

She considered her anger. It had fueled her energy in the past. Made it possible to survive on little sleep, to work a full shift or more, and still come home to make meals, do laundry, and fill the shoes of both mother and father.

However, watching Wade today, seeing him pale and tired, and knowing herself how grief ached, perhaps she could let go of her resentment towards him. Yes, he had hurt her but, for a while, he had truly loved her. She firmly believed that. However, Lord help her, how could she be expected to forgive her father or Wade's mother, the people who had caused her nothing but pain?

Seventy times seven. Jesus' admonition about the number of times to forgive goaded her conscience.

\#

Two days later, during her mother's next physical therapy appointment, Kay decided to see Wade again. This time she would not flee, no matter what he said. However, the receptionist frowned and apologized. "He says he doesn't want to see you again."

"Please, tell him I have important information for him."

"He isn't in now, but I'll relay the message." Her red lips flattened into a straight line. Kay suspected the truth lay behind the receptionist's clenched teeth.

"Please, I need to speak to him before next weekend."

A door closed behind her. "I can give him your message." Wilhelmina Hampton strode to face Kay, stopping so close that Kay had to step back. Of all people, she was the one Kay least wanted to give her message to, and the last person she wanted to witness how vulnerable she felt.

"Obviously he doesn't want to see you, Kay."

Kay turned to leave immediately, but nearly bumped into Franklin Hampton, Wade's father, as he entered the office from outdoors. "Steady there. Hello, Kay Collie. What's wrong? You look upset. Come into my office and sit. I'll get you something to drink."

"She's leaving, Franklin. She's been here to bother Wade, and he won't see her. I offered to give him whatever urgent message she thinks he needs."

"Willie, it's been years. Let the poor girl be." He guided Kay with an arm around her shoulder, talking low, as if to a frightened child. "I was sorry to hear about your father. He had become quite an accomplished artist. One of my friends had his wife's portrait done and it's beautiful."

Before Kay knew it, he steered her to a chair inside his office. Wilhelmina followed, but Franklin stopped her. "Give us some time alone, dear, please." He didn't wait for a reply, but closed the door.

Franklin Hampton was not a tall man, but his bearing made him appear so. Wade had once told her his father's gentle affability often lulled opposing attorneys into assuming he was no formidable foe. They discovered otherwise when he rose to the defense of clients others wouldn't consider. Kay had always hoped to stay on his good side. His winning track record in court left other lawyers in awe, and his reputation had made her suspect a custody case wasn't likely to go her way. Franklin had never, however, openly opposed her the way his wife did. If not for Wilhelmina ending her marriage, she thought he might have become the kind father figure she had never known.

"Would you like coffee? Water?"

When she shook her head, he dragged a chair to sit facing her, leaning forward a bit until his eyes were level with hers. "Our family owes you many apologies, Kay. Forgive me for not helping you sooner. I can stand against nearly any lawyer in this state and win an argument but I rarely stand up to Wilhelmina."

Kay tilted her head. Could she trust this man?

"My wife hasn't been a happy woman for a long time. Even before she realized the match she thought was perfect for Wade...." He shook his head and leaned back a bit. "Poor Tiffany. I tried everything I could to get her to the top of the transplant list. The sad fact is I'm a big fish but in a very little pond."

Wilhelmina opened the door to the office and stepped in, her chin raised.

Franklin registered surprise, but then he smiled. "Oh good. Mrs. Hampton can offer you her own apology. That is, if you're staying, dear." The smile disappeared and the two Hamptons stared each other down. Wilhelmina left, but slammed the door hard enough to make Kay jump.

"Now Kay. I assume you've come back to Butte to help your mother. Not, as certain people accuse, because you heard of Tiffany's poor health and you hoped to recapture my son's love. Though I suspect his heart has been yours for years."

At this, Kay's own heart leapt, but she willed it to steady. "I nursed that hope for a long time, but he didn't come to find me. And I had signed an oath to your wife that I wouldn't contact him."

"In exchange for $20,000, if I remember correctly. You're a formidable negotiator. And one who kept her word for years."

He touched the tips of his fingers together and leaned back the rest of the way in his chair. "Why?"

"Excuse me?"

"Why did you take money rather than fight for your marriage?"

Kay's mind raced. She could say she knew she wouldn't win against such a lawyer. She could say her hopes died when she saw Wade's signature. But this man's eyes demanded deeper truth. She pitied the witnesses he cross-examined.

She stood. "This conversation needs to be with Wade. Thank you for your time, Mr. Hampton."

He rose, but didn't try to stop her as she mustered her dignity and left his office.

Wilhelmina sat stiffly in the reception area, arms crossed, and foot tapping.

Neither woman spoke as Kay left. Before the door closed behind her, she heard Franklin say, "Wilhelmina, we need to talk."

She needed to talk, too—with Wade—but she wouldn't try his office again.

#

Wade stood inside the closed door of his office, biting his bottom lip. Why did Kay force him into this position? He couldn't see her. Each time he did, he lost all clarity. He wanted to wrap her in his arms and never again let go. Run his hands through her hair, kiss those lips. He had to stop this train of thought. He rested his forehead against the cool metal of the door.

He could hear his mother's rancor and then the tone of voice his father used to persuade someone. He jumped when his father's office door slammed. Wade peered into the waiting room. His mother dropped into a seat and crossed her arms. One foot began tapping. Not a good sign, especially now that she saw him.

"Wade, you look dreadful. Sit down, let me feel your forehead."

"Can't right now, Mother." He snatched his briefcase off his desk, paused to murmur to Mary, "I'll call you after my meeting to reschedule the week," then bolted through the waiting room.

He escaped out the door and hurried to his car, the fire in his mother's eyes and her "Wade Franklin Hampton, you're not well!" burning through him. He tossed the briefcase onto the passenger seat and jerked the Mustang out of the parking space. He patted his pocket and realized he left his cell phone on his desk. All the better for not being disturbed. What he needed was an escape to his cabin. He headed west.

By the time he reached Anaconda, thirty miles from Butte, the nausea that haunted him lately rose full force. Clamminess chilled his upper body. He stopped at the local drug store to buy liquid antacid and gulped half the bottle before he started to drive again.

He had hoped once the funeral was over, he'd start feeling better again. He hadn't felt well for a long time. Probably gave himself an ulcer, worrying about Tiffany. And what good had it done? She was gone. All his bargaining with God, all his promises of fidelity, all the feelings for Kay that he captured and locked down again and again. What good had any of it done? In spite of every effort, his marriage to Tiffany disintegrated. And Tiffany still died.

When things were already hard enough, he had to go find Kay and convince her to come back for her mother. *What was that all about, Jesus? Didn't you think I was tortured enough? You had to bring her here again after all these years?*

Wade remembered the way she dropped to the floor after she answered the door in Spokane. He had needed all his resistance not to enfold her in the love he had denied so long. But after she wrestled her way out of his arms and fell, he had stepped back. He had played the perfect husband, except in his heart. Jesus knew his heart, knew he had withheld part of it from Tiffany. Did she die because she needed that part? Did Jesus get even by bringing Kay back into his life?

Police lights caught Wade's attention in his rear view mirror. He glanced down at his speedometer. Eighty. How could he possibly be going eighty in a forty-five speed zone? He pulled over to the snowy shoulder of the two-lane road, powered down the window, and watched in his rear view mirror as a very tall patrolman approached.

The officer towered above the Mustang. "What's the hurry?"

"Sorry, I was upset. I didn't realize how fast I was going. I'm a couple of miles from my cabin for some days alone to clear my head.

The giant pointed to the brown bag, its top twisted around the bottle's neck. "You been drinking already today?"

Wade took the antacid out of the bag and showed the officer.

The patrolman made Wade walk the line anyway.

The nausea flared as he stared down at the white shoulder stripe, and he had to stop and close his eyes. He started again and was able, with extreme concentration, to keep his feet on the line. The officer wasn't satisfied until Wade blew into the breathalyzer and passed.

He still wrote a ticket as Wade climbed back into the car, and cautioned him. "You seem off. Drive carefully to your cabin and get some rest there."

Wade nodded and powered up the window, distracted by his feet. They felt as swollen as on a cross-country flight. Struggling around the steering wheel, he loosened his shoelaces, then eased onto the road. The patrolman followed until Wade turned onto a random driveway and waved. When the officer's car was out of sight, Wade returned to the highway and drove farther west. He had driven this road hundreds of times over the years, but this time the snowy driveways confused him. Before he recognized it, he had passed his own and needed to U-turn to get back to it.

As he got out of the car, colorful spots whirled in front of his eyes against the snow. He steadied himself until they cleared but then fought vertigo to the cabin. His body ached to lie down. He tried several keys before one opened the door. He sank into the first chair he reached. When he woke sometime later, he stood to make himself something to eat. This time blackness seemed to rush past his ears, blocking all sound except the thud of his head hitting the floor.

CHAPTER 12

Kay ended her second flight from the Hampton's office at the same McDonald's where she rinsed the tears from her face again. She tried to pray, but her greatest wish was to return to Spokane and how things were before the twins had left. What good would it do to ask for that? Instead she only managed a simple, *Help me.*

She glanced at her watch and hurried back to the physical therapist's office. The sessions tired Sadie so much that she didn't want to keep her mother waiting. Kay rushed into the clinic, but stopped short. Madge sat next to her mother, their heads together, both laughing like conspirators. Madge's hands never missed a stitch of her crocheting while they talked. Her mother didn't look as worn as she had last time she finished her therapy.

"Hello, Mom. Madge." Kay tried to keep the coolness out of her voice, but her mother's face tightened and she knew she had failed.

"Oh, Kay dear, Madge dropped by and offered to take me to lunch after my appointment."

Madge glared over her glasses at Kay. "We've been waiting for you to show up so we could go. Didn't want you to think you'd lost your mother."

Kay couldn't bear much more of this day. "Yes, I'm sure you worry about me losing her. I'm such a bad daughter after all."

Her mother stood. "Kathleen Collie!"

Kay felt tears threaten to return. She had no fight left in her. "I'm sorry, Mama. Madge, please forgive me. I'm just... Well, so much has happened. Of course you should go to lunch. Madge, you're a good friend."

Madge stood and looked Kay directly in the eyes. "And maybe you are a good daughter, Kay. I always wanted a daughter." She patted Kay's cheek, then turned and put her crocheting back in a shopping bag. "Join us?"

Kay was stunned. "No, but thank you. Maybe I'll see if Francie is free for lunch." She could use a friendship like her mother's.

Unfortunately, Francie had already eaten, so Kay promised to try again, next time her mother didn't need her. She drove back to the house. The weeks of caring for her mother had eased the animosity she felt for the place. The little bungalow almost held a homey quality. Though small by others' standards, it seemed spacious after her years of condo living.

She smiled. Her apartment-like home had forced a kind of modest life on Kay and the children. There simply wasn't room for too many material belongings. Their closets were small and storage at a premium. All three of them carefully considered bringing anything new into their home, for something old would have to go. Still, Drew had his dead computers and Dana her cages of various wounded birds and small animals. Kay's extravagance was her book collection. Once the children were old enough to be out with friends during the evenings, she had renewed her affection for reading in bed for hours at a time.

Kay entered the kitchen through the back door, still taken with the idea of reading in bed, but once in the cheery pink room she reconsidered. She had been cooking simple meals for herself and her mother since so many other details claimed time. Today seemed like an opportunity to bake. Besides, the twins would arrive in a matter of days and a full cookie jar might help with the long talks she anticipated ahead.

After a quick assessment of the cupboards, she decided on chocolate chip cookies. As Sadie and Marge returned, Kay slid the first batch out of the oven.

Madge inhaled slowly. "I think I'm back in my mama's kitchen."

The look of wistfulness on her face relaxed the tightness in Kay's shoulders that usually lasted throughout any contact with her mother's friend.

"Kay dear, if those taste as good as they smell, I won't be able to touch my toes tomorrow morning." Sadie winked at Madge, who laughed.

"Sadie, I bet you haven't touched your toes in years. I know I haven't!"

Kay's mother grinned and squatted down to show Madge how easily it was done. "Now, if you two would be so kind as to help me back up. Easy on the arm, please."

Kay and Madge rolled their eyes, then both reached out to help

Sadie to a chair. Madge took the spatula and lifted a cookie off the sheet, tossing it quickly back and forth between her fingers. "Bye now, ladies. Save me another one for tomorrow."

When she disappeared out the back door, Kay arranged some cookies onto a plate and sat down at the table with her mother.

They ate in companionable silence until Sadie broke into Kay's thoughts. "Did you talk to Wade?"

"He won't see me, Mama. I don't know what to do next."

"He'll come around. He's been through too much lately."

"We all have. But I have to talk to him before he sees the twins; Drew looks so much like him. He's always been a comfort to me that way."

"And Dana?" Does she look like you?"

Kay considered bringing in the family portrait that still lay wrapped in the trunk of her car. Her friend Brenda had not only sent the portrait of her holding her babies, but the one of the three of them taken during their senior photo shoot. She hid both pictures there as soon as they arrived, not knowing whether she would tell her mother about her family at that point. Her purse was closer, though, so she showed her mother the wallet photos.

Sadie took the pictures and studied them a long time. When she returned them to Kay, she was visibly shaken. She turned sad eyes to her daughter. "I've missed too much."

"We'll need to make up for it from now on."

"They have lives of their own now. Drew's off to Georgia soon, and then who knows where."

"But Dana will be home for holidays and summers still for a while. We'll spend time together, either here or in Spokane."

Kay looked at the pictures and swallowed. How would the twins react to all she would need to tell them? "Dana doesn't look like me. Her strawberry blonde hair isn't at all like Wade's sandy brown, either. Where did she get that?" As she returned the wallet to her purse she said, "I guess she simply looks like Dana."

"I can't wait to see her. Both of them. And to hug them. Not that I give great hugs with this sling." She raised it a bit, but winced.

"You're still hurting, aren't you, Mama?" How much longer would her mother need her? And what would it be like to leave her again?

"Heart and soul, Kay dear. Same as you, I suspect. Shoulder's nothing compared to that."

#

A short time later, Kay frowned at the kitchen calendar as she prepared a chicken for the oven. Two days until her children arrived. Two days and then she would have to share them. The phone on the wall next to the calendar rang and she jumped.

"Kay Collie," she answered, almost adding, "Fourth Floor West," as she did at work.

"Kay, Wilhelmina Hampton, here. Would you please come to the house tomorrow for brunch? Franklin and I had a long talk after you left, and I'd like to speak to you."

Kay inhaled slowly, stalling to collect her thoughts. Wade's mother was the last person she wanted to talk to. And her own mother would be left home alone.

"Please, Kay. For Wade."

Even across the phone line, Kay heard the worry in Wilhelmina's voice. What could be wrong?

"I need to help my mother for a while in the morning, but yes, I'll come. Not for brunch, though." She thought a quick visit would be wise. Lingering over a meal sounded unpleasant for all concerned.

"Fine. We'll do tea at ten. Thank you, Kay." The connection ended abruptly and Kay wondered if this might be as hard for Wilhelmina as it would be for her. Unlikely. She was probably heading into more trouble.

"Who was that, dear?" her mother asked as she padded into the kitchen in her slippers.

"Wade's mother wants me to come to tea tomorrow."

No sooner had Kay set down the phone receiver than the doorbell rang. There stood Francie at the front door with a wheeled suitcase and an odd folded chair. What now?

"Francie, what a surprise!"

"I figured Sadie would be wondering what was taking me so long. I just finished my shift at the hospital and came over."

She rolled herself and the suitcase past Kay into the living room. Sadie came in from the kitchen and giggled, "Oh, my. Is it finally my turn? I can hardly wait!"

Kay had no idea what was anticipated, but it was clear Sadie knew.

Francie rolled on into the kitchen. Kay closed the front door and followed. When Francie unfolded the chair near the sink, Sadie grinned as if Santa himself were opening his bag. She beamed at Kay. "Run get a towel, will you dear? What else do we need, Francie?"

"Two towels. We're doing Kay, too."

"How fun! Francie, you're a jewel!"

Kay put her hands on her hips. "What exactly are we doing to Kay?"

Francie only smiled and held her fingers in the stream of water under the faucet, but Sadie rocked up on her tiptoes. "It's makeover time, Kay! Francie does this for all the church members who've spent time in the hospital or who need some cheering up."

Makeover? Kay figured she was fine, thank you very much, without orange-haired Francie's help.

Her reluctance must have been obvious because her mother scowled and even stomped her foot. "Kathleen Collie, now don't you ruin this. I've looked forward to my turn for years. Of course, I was always grateful not to be the one needing cheering, but I knew when my turn came, Francie's special touch would be just the ticket."

Kay obediently fetched two towels, all the while imagining herself with orange hair. What color would her mother's white locks be turned? She figured she'd be shampooing both their heads repeatedly to be fit to show themselves in church Sunday.

When she returned to the kitchen Francie was humming and washing Sadie's hair, the older woman reclined back over the sink in the special chair.

Kay handed Francie the towel as soon as she turned off the faucet. Francie deftly wrapped Sadie's hair in a turban and helped her sit upright. A quick adjustment and the chair back stood vertical. Kay put a pot of tea on and sat at the table to watch the show.

"Sadie," Francie settled her chin into one hand, her elbow on the other, "I'm thinking you need something simple to care for. No more than a quick wash in the shower and then a little combing. To reach over your head to do curlers or blow dry would be hard on your shoulder."

"You're right, Francie. Kay's been curling my hair for me. When she goes back to work I'll be on my own."

The thought of her mother acknowledging her need to return to Spokane touched Kay. And the thought of leaving Sadie on her own made her frown.

"What, Kay? Don't you agree?"

"Sounds like a perfect idea, Mama. Francie, this is so thoughtful of you. What a wonderful ministry."

Her classmate shrugged her shoulders. "We each do what we can. I can't afford much, but I can put my beauty school training to use. The hospital job has a better benefits package than hair styling did, but I miss it and this keeps me from losing my touch."

Kay watched, mesmerized as Francie snipped and shaped her mother's hair into a simple, but becoming style. She showed her how to use a curling iron for special occasions. Next, she applied a little mascara and a rosy shade of lipstick that Sadie declared she had always wanted to try. To finish off, Francie gave Sadie a manicure and pedicure. In an hour's time, she pampered Kay's mother in ways Kay had never imagined. Sadie glowed, and Kay caught a glimpse of her mother as a young, vibrant woman.

Then it was her turn. Kay hoped to object one more time, but a glare from her mother made her surrender to Francie's reclining chair. Francie explained she was going to work a conditioner into her hair to set a bit before she washed it and Kay relaxed over the sink with her neck supported by the chair while Francie poured tea for the three of them. In twenty minutes, Francie returned to Kay and again ran the water over her fingers while adjusting the hot and cold.

The temperature of the water relaxed her scalp and Kay imagined it magically washing tension down the drain. She'd never been to a beautician, always trimming her own hair whenever it became too long to brush quickly. Luxuriating in the experience, she felt her breathing slow and her muscles relax... until bright orange suds splashed onto Francie's arm and caught Kay's attention.

She struggled to sit up. "Francie! Are you turning me orange?"

Sadie giggled and Francie guided her back down, murmuring, "It's a henna treatment, Kay. You wait and see what it does for your highlights. Your chestnut color is so pretty, but this henna will make it feel and look like silk."

Before she could object, her head was swathed in a towel turban, her back guided upright by Francie's capable hands, and the chair back adjusted to vertical. Francie rubbed her hair gently with the towel, then continued the massage down her neck and across her shoulders. Kay melted into the experience and surrendered to whatever further gifts Francie would bestow.

In less than an hour Francie had instructed Kay in the blow dry care of her new style, shaped her nails and painted the tips white and the rest a soft pink in what Francie declared a perfect French manicure. The final gift was a foot rub that left Kay knowing exactly how a kitten feels when it purrs.

When she finally examined herself in a mirror, she beheld a Kay with soft curls and laughing eyes. This Kay was the attractive woman who had been overshadowed first as a wary teen and then as a harried mom. A Kay who hadn't appeared in many years, and even back then only with Wade.

The two Collie women felt so elegant that they considered dining out, but the roast chicken aroma emanating from the oven settled the matter. They insisted Francie join them for dinner, and she entertained them both with the stories of makeovers that had gone bad. Before they realized it, the clock struck ten. Francie rose and hugged Sadie saying,

"You're beautiful, Sadie." Then she turned to Kay. "And so are you, Kay. Amazing how much letting someone else do for you agrees with you."

Kay accompanied her friend to the door and whispered, "Francie, four years is long enough. I think you should try to be part of your daughters' lives again. You've learned from your mistakes and deserve another chance. You're missing out on too much and so are they."

Francie eyed her steadily a moment but didn't respond. Kay's own words chided her conscience and saddened her. Wade had also missed out on his children's lives and they on their father's.

They hugged and Francie whispered, "Don't you go disappearing again." Kay closed the door and exhaled deeply. She returned to the kitchen.

"She's right," Sadie said. "You seem so much more relaxed. You know, letting others help you is like giving them a gift. Or a blessing. It doesn't mean you aren't capable."

Kay felt too mellow to disagree.

#

The next morning Kay's feet dragged up the driveway to the Hampton home. The last time Kay had come to this house she wore Wade's class ring on her left hand and they were anticipating telling his parents about their marriage. No less apprehensive now, she chided herself. An adult with a successful life, she didn't need their approval.

Anxious to get this over with, but hopeful it could somehow help her talk to Wade, she squared her shoulders and rang the bell. Wilhelmina answered immediately and Kay realized she must have been watching for her.

"Kay, come in, please."

Those were the words Kay longed to hear nineteen years ago. *Kay, come in. Be part of our family.*

While Wilhelmina hung her coat, Kay took in her surroundings. The furniture wasn't the same, but the effect of texture, color, and placement still gave an impression of dignity and affluence. Oatmeal-colored carpet set off the rich brown leather side chairs and coordinated with the plush cream sofa. Throw pillows and an afghan matched the exact moss green in the landscape painting hung above the fireplace.

As Kay sat on the edge of the sofa, she realized she had positioned herself for flight. She forced herself to sit back while Wilhelmina took a seat opposite her, obviously gathering her thoughts as she poured tea for both of them.

"Kay, I haven't been myself since Sharon died."

Nineteen years was a long time to not be oneself, Kay thought.

"When you showed up at the hospital wearing Sharon's dress," Wilhelmina said, "what little reserve of strength I had left collapsed."

"I felt horrible about that. It certainly wasn't planned to upset you. I left my home, uh, suddenly."

"In my better moments, I realized that. I think I hated you for being alive to wear her clothes while Sharon lay dying."

Kay looked down. What could she say? She thought what it would be like to sit by Dana's side, knowing she was dying, and then to see someone in her clothes, vibrant and glowing from newlywed bliss. She met Wade's mother's eyes. "I'm sorry, Wilhelmina. I'm sorry Sharon died, and that Wade wasn't with you after her accident because he was with me."

Wilhelmina gave a slow, thoughtful nod. "Yes, that was part of it, too. I couldn't lose both my children."

Instead, I lost my husband, Kay thought, but clenched the words behind her teeth.

"When Sharon died, that day at her funeral, I had been… Let's just say I wasn't at my best. I'm not proud of convincing Wade to sign the annulment. I manipulated him into it, letting him think he could give me some peace, buy some time…"

"You had no right to end our marriage." Kay's words couldn't convey the depth of pain Wilhelmina had caused her.

"You made it possible. I couldn't have done it without you leaving. You sold your marriage and by doing so proved us right about you."

Kay stood to leave. Wilhelmina winced. "I'm sorry. Please sit. Never mind that now."

Kay remained standing but didn't move toward the door. She crossed her arms. "How can I not mind it? Isn't that the whole problem between us?"

"I need your help." Wilhelmina bunched the napkin that lay in her lap, then flattened it carefully again. Kay waited, curious about why Wilhelmina Hampton could possibly need help.

"Sit down, please. You make me nervous hovering over me. This isn't easy for me, you know."

Kay sat. She took a sip of her tea, all the while watching her adversary over the rim of the cup.

"Wade is despondent."

"He lost his wife. Of course he is."

"No. Yes, of course he is now. But he has been for a long time. He and Tiffany never had an easy marriage. He wanted children so badly.

We all did. All except Tiffany. Ever since she learned about her heart trouble, she gave up on that dream."

"Wade told you this?" Kay couldn't quite picture the Wade she had loved complaining to his mother about his marriage. Especially since Tiffany seemed to be everything Wilhelmina would have wanted for her son. A society lady.

"No," Wilhelmina said. "He never once complained. Tiffany told her mother everything."

"And her mother is a friend of yours and you wheedled it out of her?"

"Don't judge me. If you were a mother you'd know a mother would do anything—"

Kay nodded. "Anything to help her child."

Wilhelmina raised her eyebrows. "Yes, exactly."

The two regarded each other carefully, and Kay feared she had said too much.

Wilhelmina dismissed whatever she had been thinking with a wave of the hand. "Kay, Wade loved you once. Franklin and I admit it was wrong of us to come between you. We apologize. We need you to help him."

Kay stood again. "You are granting me permission to see Wade? Releasing me from my promise not to contact him? You still think you can control his life, and mine, don't you?"

"Maybe you can help him to feel joy again. I don't know what you think of him now, after being away so long, but if you are still hurt and angry, blame me. It was my fault. He was trying to ease my pain."

"And I was the sacrifice he offered to make peace."

Wilhelmina took a slow drink of tea, set the cup down, and stood. "He's not answering my calls. I'm frightened. I have this feeling, this premonition that I'm going to lose him. I'd rather it be to you, Kay Collie, than to despair. Please, you have medical background, if I'm not mistaken. See if you think he's ill. Report back to me."

Kay stood, feeling dismissed. The fact that Wilhelmina knew she had a medical background would need to be pursued another time. "I need to talk to him, but he won't see me. How can I do anything until he will?"

Wilhelmina walked to an elegant, dark cherry writing table and stroked the wood. "Wade made this for me." She took a paper out of a drawer and turned, business-like again. "This is a map to his cabin out at the lake. I haven't heard from him since your visit to the office. I'm guessing he's there."

Kay figured a newly widowed man wouldn't be cheered by anyone, especially her, but she needed to tell him about his children. Maybe that would help him, knowing he had a daughter and son. He'd probably hate her more for keeping them from him, but if he could get past the anger, or blame her and not hold it against them, they could be good for each other.

She took the map. "I'll go see him."

Wilhelmina blinked twice and frowned. Kay knew what it would cost her to ask for help if she were in Wilhelmina's position. But Wilhelmina wasn't the only one who would go to any lengths for her children.

CHAPTER 13

Once home again, Kay was relieved to see her mother had been fine for the hour she was out. However, a drive to the lake would take all afternoon. How could she possibly be gone that long?

Kay sat down next to her mother, who still needed help dressing and wasn't up to cooking yet. She told her about her talk with Wade's mother while at the same time noting the house around her. So much needed to be done. She asked, "Mama, how did you do it all those years, taking care of Dad, working, and cleaning the house?"

"The same way you managed school, a job, and twins by yourself, I imagine. I learned to accept any help offered and to ask when no offers came."

"I did need help at times," Kay said, "but tried everything I could before I admitted it. I traded childcare with a day-shift nurse when I first worked afternoons. It still frustrates me when I can't manage on my own."

"Time to get over that, Kay. We all need help occasionally, and we all give help when we can. What goes around comes around. Now, give someone else a chance to be the helper. Call Agnes, she offered to come over when we need her, and she's sincere."

Yes, Agnes. Maybe she could let Agnes help. The woman was all kindness and smiles. She couldn't have asked Madge, who would look down her nose the whole time.

But, when she finally forced herself to dial, Agnes wasn't available. "I'm truly sorry, Kay, I would have loved to have a whole afternoon with your mom. Wait."

Kay heard muffled murmuring as if the receiver had been covered with a hand.

"Kay, dear, Madge is here and says she'll be right over."

Kay's shoulders dropped. Yet she didn't have much choice. She needed to talk to Wade as soon as possible. "Tell her I appreciate it, Agnes. And thank you, too."

She hung up the phone, sighing with resignation. "Madge was there, Mom. She's on her way."

"Wonderful!" Sadie looked like Dana used to when a play date had been arranged.

"Yeah, wonderful. Madge will love seeing your daughter skipping out on you again."

"Nonsense. You're winning her over." Sadie exaggerated a wink and Kay couldn't help but laugh.

#

Kay started her car with a sense of urgency. She had to make Wade listen and agree to meet the twins. She didn't hold out any hope of him forgiving her. She prayed her children would understand how frightened she had been of losing them to Wilhelmina.

Kay drove west to Anaconda. The little town had been her high school's archrival, and as a teen she couldn't understand why anyone would choose to live in such a small, old community. With adult eyes now, she realized that Anaconda's commercial buildings were no older than Butte's, most built in the 1880s. She could even appreciate the small-town charm as she remembered the little central commons where she and Wade once ice-skated under the lights of a towering Christmas tree.

As she drove into Anaconda, Kay thought about her friend Francie and the husband who cared for their daughters alone in this town. What would life have been like if Kay's mom had that courage and determination when she was small? They could have lived without the fear and shame that her father's alcoholism caused. Or even if her mom had been willing to leave when Kay did, Sadie would have known her grandchildren and raising them would have been a shared endeavor.

But poor Francie, now, living without her children. Kay believed the saddest loss would be to lose a child, yet it must be even worse for Francie, losing two and knowing it was her fault. No wonder she continued to accept being apart from them. She had endangered them and could neither forgive herself nor allow herself the joy of reuniting with them. She probably felt she didn't deserve that happiness. Kay's heart could ache for her friend, but she couldn't extend that empathy towards her father. Losing her had been what he deserved.

She waited at a red light.

And yet, he had changed, from what her mother and the townspeople said of her dad. Like Francie had changed. So much unfairness.

The light turned green and, rather than proceed, she parked the car.

It was too late for her to forgive her father, but must it be too late for Francie's husband and daughters to forgive Francie?

Her thoughts turned to Wade. Hadn't she kept his children from him like Francie's husband was doing to Francie? But Wade would have been a great father and never would have endangered their children. She began to realize the ache Francie felt would be the same pain Wade would have felt if he had known about the twins. She had caused that pain, not because he would endanger the children, that would have been understandable, but because his parents might have been able to take her twins away from her. And what then? They'd have had opportunities she couldn't give them, a father who would have adored them, and two sets of doting grandparents.

Her determination to keep her children now seemed a bit less noble than it had for all the struggling years of single parenting. She realized she was finally doing what she should have done long ago. Children have a right to both parents, assuming the parents won't hurt them. Wade had the right to know and love his children. A right she'd stolen, much like Wilhelmina had stolen her marriage. It was too late for Wade to experience the joys of raising children, but it wasn't too late for Francie.

Though she felt an urgency to get to Wade, her dread of the moment when she'd confess her secret and his predictable angry reaction made her ask what difference a short postponement would make. She glanced around where she had parked, wishing for the days of phone booths with phone books. Instead, she made her way into the hardware store. In whatever trade Allen Shea worked with his brother-in-law, the hardware store would know him and how she could find him.

Fifteen minutes later a nice looking man in a plaid woolen jacket approached her at a picnic table in the park. She would have preferred to meet him in the warmth of a café. Anaconda proved every bit as cold as Butte this time of year, but she wanted to talk to him in private and small town cafés were never private.

She stood, introduced herself, and offered him the coffee she'd bought him. They would need the help to stay warm.

"I remember you, Kay," Allen said as he sat and warmed his hands around the cup. "You were one of the quiet, studious girls in high school."

"I was Francie's biology partner," she replied, and watched him drop eye contact while his face tightened in what? Anger? Pain? She continued, "Francie's been a big help to me since I came back to Butte."

He met her eyes now, with "none of your business" written all over his face.

She plowed on anyway. "Allen, I admire your decision to take the girls away. I think it was the right thing to do."

His look changed to surprise. "I didn't expect that from you."

"I grew up with an alcoholic." The admission—speaking the forbidden—surprised her, but so did the realization that it made her feel strong. She held eye contact. "I wish my mom had taken me away from my dad."

He nodded and visibly relaxed. "I couldn't risk her hurting them. She'd vowed over and over that she had stopped drinking. Then over and over I'd find out she'd lied. When the police called about the accident, it was the last straw." He shook his head slowly as if he still couldn't believe it. "She'd jeopardized my girls' lives, and I swore I'd never allow her to do that again.

"The first months were rough. The girls cried every night for their mother." The hardness in his voice suddenly softened. "You see, when she was sober she was a really sweet mom." His eyes focused far off and he looked wistful.

Kay could see he was remembering better times. "She would be a sweet mom again," she said gently.

Immediately his face hardened, his lips pressed together, and he leaned back.

Kay hurried, worried he would stop listening. "She's been sober ever since she went to jail."

He rolled his eyes.

"Truly, four years. She goes to church, she's holding down a respectable job. She's been so kind to my mother since she fell."

Allen appeared suddenly fascinated by his coffee cup.

"Did you know she has her own personal ministry?" she asked.

This caught his attention and his eyes met Kay's breifly.

She continued, "Whenever any of her church member ladies have been in the hospital or have suffered a loss, she goes to visit them and gives them a makeover."

He cocked his head.

"I know that might not seem cool to a guy, but to the women who benefit from her attention, it's heaven. She brightens their moods in spite of what they've been through. You can't know how feeling pretty again can renew a woman's spirit." It had done that for her mother and for Kay herself, she realized. "People look forward to her visit like a light to brighten their dark hours."

Allen looked a bit less sure of himself, so Kay reached across the table and touched his arm. "I did what you've done. I took children away from their father, and for a reason not nearly as noble as yours. But now they want to know their father and when they do, I'm afraid they'll resent my decision to cheat them out of a relationship with him for all these years. I don't know if they will ever forgive me."

She drew her hand back. "I don't want that for you or for your girls. Please, give Francie a chance. Get to know her again, and only if you see that what I've said is true, then let the girls back into her life. If you don't, if I'm wrong, then you'll have a clear conscience when the girls are bigger and ask why you've continued to keep them away."

She stood. "People can change. My dad did, though I never would have believed it."

Kay shook Allen's hand and thanked him for coming to hear her out. As she returned to her car, she knew personally how hard it would be for Allen because she was facing the same challenge. He risked being disappointed one more time, though she truly didn't think he would be. She risked losing her children, not physically like she had feared all these years, but emotionally.

However, she had agreed it was time for them to meet their dad. Beyond time for him to know about them. As she drove out of the park to head west, both the sense of urgency and the sense of dread returned.

#

Kay drove through pleasant neighborhoods and out the other side of Anaconda, now following Wilhelmina's map. Thirteen more miles west brought her to the first of two lakes. Silver Lake gave way to Georgetown Lake, where the better-off people like the Hamptons from both Butte and Anaconda owned summer cabins. Glancing at the map one more time, she found the turn she needed and drove down a snow-rutted driveway toward the lake.

At the back of the cabin, a shiny blue Mustang reminded her of the older red one they drove to Idaho to elope. She parked her car and followed the only set of snowy footprints to the front door. As she rounded the corner, the scenery caught her breath. Frosted lodge pole pines marched in open formation down toward the crystal blue lake. The far shore met pine-covered hills, dotted with chimneys reaching up in stunted imitation of the trees.

The view encouraged her, and she whispered a prayer of thanksgiving for its beauty. She continued her prayer with a request for help to get through to Wade and to bless the meeting of the small family she and he had created. Her legs trembled a bit on the three steps to the porch as she tried to imagine leaving her worries at God's door.

No one answered her knock. She knew Wade must be home or nearby, since his car was there and the surrounding snow was unbroken by any more footprints. She knocked again, but the cabin was small and she was sure the first knock would have been heard. She turned back toward the lake and called, "Wade? Wade Hampton?"

No answer.

She felt her cheeks warm at her next thought, and she glanced around to make sure no one was watching. Then she cupped her hands around her eyes to block the lake's reflection and peered through the window.

Wade lay motionless on the floor, his hand reaching out toward the door.

Kay's heart began pumping adrenaline. She whispered another *thank you* when she found the door unlocked and dropped to Wade's side. Nurse experience took over. He didn't respond to his name or her touch. His pulse was weak. She pried open an eyelid, while telling the unconscious Wade exactly what she was doing.

Kay yanked her cell phone from her pocket. No reception.

She looked around the cabin but didn't see a phone. She ran to the porch and called, "Help! Can anybody hear me? I need help!"

No response.

But Kay's training from nursing school had taught her enough. She grabbed Wade's arm and wrestled him into a sitting position, until she could wedge her shoulder under his ribs.

"Don't leave me." His words were weak, but relief washed over her to hear them.

"I won't, I promise." His weight staggered her, but she stumbled and lurched with him towards her car. Half dragging, half shoving, she wedged him into the back seat. She felt badly about how uncomfortable his folded body looked, but she didn't have time to reposition him. She maneuvered until she could fasten a seatbelt across his hips and then jumped behind the wheel.

"Wade, you stay with me, you hear? I'm taking you to a hospital. I'm not leaving you. I'll be right there until you get the help you need." He didn't answer her, but it kept her mind focused to talk to him. "What were you doing out here alone? You must have known you needed treatment?"

She sped back toward Anaconda as fast as her car and the sanded road would allow. She hoped a highway patrol would stop her and radio ahead for help, but she didn't see one. Given the size of Montana and its sparse population, the chance of seeing law enforcement was small. She'd have to rely on God's help.

"Wade, why did you come out here alone? Why now? I want you to meet your children, Wade. You have to hold on to see them. You'll be so proud of them. The twins are eighteen and they're good kids. Drew, he looks like you. Or rather, like you did when we got married. He's in the Army and coming to see you on leave next weekend.

"And Dana, she's starting college and you'd have a crush on her if you were her age—and not her father, of course. Dana's beautiful. I don't know where she got her strawberry blonde hair. Her eyes are blue. I didn't expect that since mine are green and yours are the most beautiful brown I've ever seen. She wants to be a doctor like I always did. I had to give that up for the twins' sake but she'll be a wonderful, caring physician."

Kay glanced at Wade in the rear view mirror frequently but he showed no signs of rousing. She noted his skin tone and couldn't believe she had missed the symptoms.

"God, help us!" She continued to talk aloud to keep her mind from racing faster than she could drive. "Help Wade to be all right. He has to meet the twins. They have to know their father. I was a fool to try to do it all on my own. I was so afraid of losing them like I lost him. They all needed each other."

She glanced at the mirror again. "Wade, we're almost there. You hang on. We have so much to catch up on. I know you might not forgive me, but you're going to love your son and daughter."

When she neared Anaconda's city limits, she tried her cell phone again, dialing 911. An emergency team waited in the hospital driveway when she arrived.

"I found him barely conscious thirty minutes ago, weak pulse, eyes…" she stopped at the look the doctor gave her.

"Patient's name?"

"Wade Hampton." He started checking Wade's vital signs as soon as orderlies had lifted him onto the gurney. Kay hurried to keep up with the team as they moved toward the emergency room.

"How long have his symptoms been this severe?"

"I don't know."

"Has he been receiving dialysis?"

"I don't know."

"Who's his attending physician?"

When she didn't answer, he stopped and eyed her suspiciously.

"You are?"

"Kay Collie."

"Relative?"

Kay paused only a second. "His wife." She hadn't spoken those words in years, but they felt right and true.

The doctor glanced at her ring finger. She dug quickly into the zipper pocket of her purse and found the wedding band, showing it to him as she slid it on.

The doctor's expression didn't soften. "Yeah, my wife always hides her ring in her purse when she's around me. I'm sorry but I'll need to restrict my comments to his family. Contact them."

She couldn't believe he'd take time for nitpicking. "Wade graduated from Butte High, same year as me. He was a track star and on the swim team. He's a lawyer now in his father's firm. His parents are Franklin—"

The doctor cut her off with a raised hand. "Franklin Hampton? I'm definitely not going to discuss this with you. He could sue the stethoscope right off me."

Kay grasped his arm. "Please, I have proof." She ran to the car and grabbed the wrapped portrait of the babies. She tore into the paper, removing the back of the frame as quickly as her shaking fingers allowed her. At last she withdrew the document she had hidden there and hurried back into the emergency room. The doctor ignored her and fired orders to the scrub-clad nurses. Kay pushed her marriage certificate under the doctor's nose.

He studied it briefly, then studied her.

She met his gaze evenly. "I was away. But I'm back. I am his wife."

The doctor nodded. "Call the rest of his family. I'll come to you in the waiting room when I can."

Kay acquiesced and hurried to the waiting room. People filled most of the chairs and a television chattered loudly. She needed air, so she went outside to make the phone calls she dreaded.

"Franklin, this is Kay Collie. When I found Wade at his cabin, he was on the floor barely conscious. You and Wilhelmina need to come to the Anaconda hospital."

The second and third calls were even more difficult, but her knowledge from years of nursing experience forced her hand. "Fly to Butte immediately. Your father might be dying. Someone will meet you at the airport and bring you to us."

She called her mother next, but talked to Madge because her mother was napping. Madge took charge. "You stay as long as you need to, Kay. I'll make sure someone from the church meets the flights and bring your twins to you. Your mom will want to be at your side. I'll bring her there myself and home again when her energy gives out."

Kay thanked her and returned to wait. This wasn't the way it was supposed to happen. Wade and the children were supposed to meet after she had time alone to explain her decisions, to ask them to try to understand that she did the best she could. Maybe over dinner in the newfound comfort of her childhood home. Not here in this cold, frightening place.

A nurse called her name. She followed the efficient brunette who spoke over her shoulder at Kay. "He's asking for you. Only stay a minute, though."

Kay entered his cubicle in ICU and with a glance at the monitors and tubes assured herself that Wade was receiving proper care. She took his hand and his eyes opened. He struggled to speak so she leaned close to his mouth.

"I heard you," he whispered. "About not leaving. About our kids."

Kay groaned.

He squeezed her hand weakly. "Promise me you won't tell anyone if I need a kidney."

So he knew how sick he was. There was no way she'd promise that.

She couldn't break a promise and she couldn't let him die. But if the twins could save his life, it might jeopardize their own. She knew her children. Drew joined the Army out of a drive to risk himself for the good of others. And Dana, how many injured animals had she nursed to health? But if they inherited their father's condition and had already given him one of their kidneys... Could she risk one of her children for this man whom she had loved completely, but who turned away when she needed him?

He squeezed her hand harder. "Kay, I've made the doctor promise not to tell. Please, swear you won't."

Kay heard his heart monitor beeps increase as his agitation grew. He needed to stay calm. What else could she do?

"I promise."

He released her hand and slipped out of consciousness.

CHAPTER 14

Kay paced and prayed in the waiting room until Wilhelmina and Franklin rushed in, her face pale and his flushed. They spotted Kay and hurried to her.

"What happened? What did they say?"

"Wade's been sick for quite some time now. Didn't you know about it?" Surely, they must have known.

His mother's eyebrows tilted toward each other. "I knew something was wrong, but I didn't know what. We've been focused on Tiffany. His color has been off and he's looked exhausted, but we assumed it was from worrying about her."

"What exactly is the diagnosis?" Franklin's voice took on the courtroom tone that had caused Kay to leave his office, only days ago.

"The doctor said he would talk to us when he could."

Franklin pressed. "You've been a nurse for years. Surely you know something,"

Kay felt cornered. It wasn't her place to make diagnoses, though her suspicion had been right. They probably wouldn't believe her anyway.

Her thoughts stopped short. "Yesterday Wilhelmina mentioned my medical training. Now this. How did you know I've been a nurse, and worked in Spokane?"

Franklin shook his head like a dog pestered by a fly. "What does that matter now? Wade must have told me."

"Wade didn't know. He would have come to me if he had." She crossed her arms. When he didn't respond, she began to tap her toe.

Wilhelmina sat in the closest chair. She touched her husband's arm and he took a seat next to her. "Sit, Kay," she said, "and we'll explain without bothering the rest of the room."

Kay uncrossed her arms. She settled herself opposite them.

"Institutions used to be more careless with personal information than they are now. I hired an investigator who found your registration in the nursing program in Spokane. Periodically I asked him to verify your registration and, after you graduated, your employment. I'm not proud of myself. When it became obvious you weren't coming back, we stopped."

"Wade didn't know?"

"Of course not. The lovesick boy would have been at your side in a minute," Wilhelmina said.

Kay couldn't believe she had been willing to help this woman. Still, because of Wilhelmina's premonition, Kay had driven to the cabin and found Wade. She hoped she had arrived in time. In time to buy him more time. She reminded herself that they all shared love for Wade. Realizing they still waited for her to respond, she took a deep breath and prayed quickly for guidance.

"My guess is Wade is suffering from acute kidney dysfunction. He might have died if he'd been alone at the cabin any longer. But like you said, I'm a nurse,"—*not a doctor, thanks to you,* she thought—"and you should wait to hear from his physician."

Like both Wade's parents, she sat back, all three alone with their thoughts. Twice Franklin asked at the reception desk to see his son, but was told he was having tests done.

A half hour passed. Madge and Sadie found their way to the little group and Kay told them what she had told Wade's parents. Sadie sat on Kay's left and Kay held on to her mother's good hand, knowing they prayed silently together, and fairly certain that Madge was storming heaven with her opinions, too. Wilhelmina clutched Franklin's arm, the anxiety clearly written on their faces.

Finally, the doctor approached them. Kay introduced him to the others. He shook hands all around, then led them to a small glassed-in corner of the waiting room and closed the door.

"Mr. Hampton is in critical condition. The next few hours will be pivotal. He has not regained consciousness since shortly after he was brought in by his—"

Kay's eyes widened and met the doctor's with a silent plea.

"—by Ms. Collie," he continued. "I'm afraid I am not ..." He paused and Kay knew he chose his words carefully, "able... to offer you much hope."

Kay had known, but his words still caused her to touch the glass wall to steady herself. Sadie whispered a soft, "Oh dear." Wilhelmina buried her face in her hands and sobbed. Franklin's face flushed redder before he turned away to comfort his wife.

"You may see him, one or two at a time, but he's in critical condition and needs no disturbances."

Kay realized the tension between them was so palpable that the doctor had sensed it. She nodded at him and thanked him as he left the dazed group.

After a little while, Madge and Sadie murmured to each other and stood. Sadie hugged her daughter. "Don't you worry about me. I have my friends and I'll be fine. You take care of Wade," she gestured toward the Hamptons with her eyes, "and yourself." She nodded at Wade's parents, but they were in their own world of misery and didn't seem to notice her leave. Madge patted Kay's forearm as she shadowed Sadie out of the room.

Kay jumped and caught up with her mother. "Mama," she dropped her voice, "Dana and Drew are on their way. Can they stay with you after they leave here?" Another introduction that she wouldn't be able to orchestrate.

"I wouldn't want it any other way, dear."

#

By 10 p.m. Kay and the Hamptons had alternated several turns in the ICU with Wade, though he hadn't awakened again. Luckily, they were with him and Kay was in the waiting room when her children arrived, escorted by Francie and a plaid-jacketed man Kay now knew to be Allen. Even in the midst of her fears, seeing Francie with Allen made her smile. But having her children within reach brought sheer joy. Kay and the twins held each other in the familiar embrace Drew used to initiate by extending his arms to Kay and Dana and yelling, "Group hug!"

Francie beamed Kay a grin when the twins stepped back. "Thank you," she said to Kay as she motioned with her head toward the man who had hung back a bit. "I hear you've met Allen. We're talking. And I'll be praying for you and Wade. Nice kids, by the way."

"Thanks for the ride, Francie and Allen!" Dana called as the couple disappeared out the door.

Kay wanted to savor the moment while her twins were all still her own. Drew wore his fatigues. His shoulders were filling out and he seemed taller since the last time she saw him. Dana wore a Seattle T-shirt and jeans. Her face held a bright confidence, despite the worry in her eyes. Kay felt such relief at seeing them that she nearly succumbed to the tears she had held in check.

"Mom, we can't stand it much longer. Tell us everything." Drew's face showed concerned for her, but she heard frustration in his voice.

Kay led her children, two anxious young adults, into the glass room and closed the door. "Sit," she ordered, "this is a long story."

Emotions kaleidoscoped on their faces as she started from her abusive childhood, talked of meeting Wade in high school, and covered their elopement right after graduation. The hardest to tell was the story of the days that followed. She didn't want to turn her children against any of the Hamptons, even Wilhelmina. She selected her words with great care.

"When we returned from our little honeymoon, we discovered your Aunt Sharon, your dad's sister, had been in a car accident. She died a few weeks later, and grief caused us all to make mistakes. Your dad signed annulment papers. I was your age but had to make quick decisions all by myself. I knew I was pregnant, but I was too hurt and afraid to tell anyone. I left.

"You two know about the following years. Then days after I took Dana to college, your dad showed up on our doorstep." She took a deep breath and both twins started to ask a question, but she held up her hand. "There's not enough time now, but I promise I'll answer all your questions soon.

"Your Grandma Sadie—that's my mom—has only known about you two for a few days. I'm told my dad, your Grandpa Stu, changed when I left. It sounds like you would have been proud to know him, but he died a few weeks ago. I'm sorry you missed the chance to know that grandfather, but there are two more grandparents who don't know about you. We need to fix that tonight. First though, you need to meet your dad. He's in intensive care from a complication of diabetes. Before he lost consciousness, I told him about you."

Kay's voice broke. "I'm praying for two things tonight. That he'll live long enough to love you two as much as I do, and that you'll forgive me for my mistakes."

She stretched out her arms, "Group hug?"

Beyond the shoulders of her huddled children, she could see Wade's parents coming back into the waiting room. They returned to their seats, their worries keeping them from noticing Kay and the twins.

She led the way to the ICU, trying to see the scene as it would appear to her children. Tubes and monitors distracted attention from the unconscious man in the bed. "Dana and Drew, this is your father, Wade Hampton." She shook her head as she looked at Wade, motionless in the bed. "I'll leave you two with him. It's possible he can hear you."

She waited in the hall outside the ICU, not wanting to open herself to questions from the older Hamptons quite yet.

While she waited, words replayed in her mind, conversations with Wade, Sadie, and Brenda.

"Promise me you won't tell them if I need a kidney."

"Love always requires sacrifice…"

"Sometimes we must break a promise to protect the most vulnerable."

"Family secrets can allow horrible things to continue."

"God is surely working in your life, Kay. He has plans for you, good plans."

But Wilhelmina's words haunted her most: *"If you had ever been a mother you'd know a mother would do anything—"*

"Anything to help her child."

Wilhelmina had done everything she could when she thought she was losing Wade, right after losing her daughter. Kay had worked herself ragged ever since then, rather than risk losing her children. Now Wade's only hope was a kidney from an immediate family member. A kidney that their child might need to overcome this disease if it struck one of them. She had promised not to tell and she never broke a promise, but she was sick of secrets. Yet, she feared both her children would accept the risk if they knew.

Would she gamble her son or daughter's life for the man she still loved? If she did, would that make her like her mother, who put her husband ahead of her child?

There was a difference, though. Her children were adults. When she became an adult, she chose for herself and left. They deserved the right to decide for themselves. And now, when the chance to know their father might be lost, she regretted that she had kept him from them. If she didn't break her promise to Wade, they would probably never know him.

She sifted through the chatter in her mind, hearing the echoes of her own, "I promise." She settled instead on the words of her mother, "Sometimes we must break a promise to protect the most vulnerable."

When Dana and Drew emerged from ICU, she took one of their hands in each of hers and searched their eyes. "How are you two doing?"

Drew stared down at the floor. Dana met her mother's gaze through tears. "This is really hard, Mom. We might not ever get to know our dad. I wish you'd told us earlier."

Drew nodded and Kay could feel his frustration rise like a wall between them. He dropped her hand. "We had a right to know Dad, even if you two were separated."

Dana put her hand on her brother's shoulder. "Later, Drew."

"No, too much has been put off for later. Were you so angry with him that you were willing to let us do without a dad?"

"No, that wasn't it!" Kay reached out but Drew stepped back. She lowered her hand, then rubbed her other arm with it. "I was afraid I'd lose you both."

Drew tilted toward her, his voice low but outraged. "You chose your fear over our rights!"

Kay had never seen Drew this angry, but she couldn't wait until he had cooled off. "There's more you should know."

Her children looked at her, incredulous, and Kay knew what they must be thinking. They had learned about their mother's past and her secrets. They'd met a father who might be dying. Two grandparents sat in the waiting room, strangers to them. And yet, there could be more?

Kay wanted desperately to take away the pain in the eyes of these two beloved faces. Instead, she would have to inflict more.

"Wade... your dad... made me swear not to tell you something. But I don't want any more secrets. And a decision has to be made that only you two can make. Your dad needs a kidney. If one of you two qualifies, you could save his life."

The two reacted in opposite ways, much as they always had.

"A transplant?" Dana's pre-med passions colored her voice with enthusiasm.

"Surgery?" Drew visibly fought to control his fear. He glanced at his sister, then back over his shoulder into his father's room.

Kay watched the boy do mental battle and emerge a soldier and a man. He wouldn't choose fear over the life of others. For an instant, she hoped neither twin would be a match. Maybe Wade's parents? No, even though she felt justified as a mother to tell her children, she had no right to tell Wade's parents what he didn't want anyone to know. And his parents were older. Surgery would be harder on them than on one of her children.

The twins turned toward each other and communicated without words. Dana faced her mother. "How do we start?"

Kay's heart skipped a beat and her mouth went dry. "First, we introduce you to your grandparents. Then I'll ask for the tests to be run." She turned to one, then the other. "Are you sure?"

Drew nodded. "We're sure."

Kay brought them to meet their father's parents, one arm around each. She could feel the tension in Drew's shoulders. She stopped in front of the Hamptons. Franklin and Wilhelmina stood.

"Franklin and Wilhelmina, I'd like to introduce you to your grandchildren." Wilhelmina jolted back and covered her mouth with her hand. Franklin put his arm around her to steady her. "Dana and Drew are Wade's children, grown up from when they were beautiful twin babies, born one month premature, eight months after our wedding day. My children are willing to try to save your son's life, if either qualifies as a kidney donor."

The older couple seemed too stunned to speak. Then Franklin withdrew his arm from his wife's back and reached out to shake Drew's hand. Wilhelmina whispered, "Your hair, it's exactly like Sharon's before she bleached it." She embraced Dana and began to cry on her shoulder.

Kay left the four of them together and hurried to talk to the receptionist. Tests were needed *stat* to see if either child would match as a donor. Because Wade was still unconscious, she signed permission forms for surgery, as his next of kin. *So sue me,* she thought. *As long as we give Wade every chance we can, I'll take whatever comes.*

Dear God, protect him AND our children.

When she returned to the group, their conversation was nervous and halting, but all eyes shone.

#

Not only was Drew a match, but a transplant surgeon was visiting Anaconda for the long weekend, planning to enjoy the local Jack Nicklaus golf course. Before Drew had time to reconsider his decision, he, the surgeon, and Wade were transported by helicopter to the larger Butte hospital. Kay, Dana, and the Hamptons followed by car. Drew was already prepped for surgery when Kay arrived. She held his hand, fighting to stay brave in front of her son. He hadn't met her eyes since his decision, and she figured his anger hadn't burned out yet.

"Mom, I could be discharged from the service because of this."

Since junior high, his dream had been to join the military. Kay had barely been able to keep him from enlisting before graduation. She squeezed his hand even tighter.

"Maybe so. But you'll be a hero, anyway, you know. Sometimes our dreams have to change."

"It's hard to believe how much life can change in a day."

She nodded, recalling numerous such days. When she confirmed she was pregnant. The day her marriage was signed away. When her twins were born. Finding Wade on her condo doorstep. Seeing him lying on the floor of his cabin.

She pushed away the image. "Thank you, Drew, for being so brave. I've always loved your dad, even through years of being angry with him. He's a good man. Like you." She kissed his forehead and stepped aside as an attendant pushed the bed toward the operating room.

It took all her self-control not to yell, "Stop! Don't do this!" Should a son have to risk his life for a man he never knew, even if the man is his father? But Drew had made that decision, and she was left behind to struggle with extremes of fear, regret, and gratitude.

A second gurney wheeled toward her with Wade, still unconscious. She stopped the attendant and kissed the love of her life on the cheek. "God bless and keep you both safe," she whispered. "And please, forgive me."

The double doors close silently behind them, and she knew the best she could do now was return to the waiting room and pray.

As she rounded the corner into that room, she stopped short. The sun was beginning to stream through the windows. Wilhelmina dozed, her cheek against Franklin's right shoulder. Dana lay asleep with her coppery head resting on her sweatshirt, bunched against her grandfather's left knee. He looked at Kay, then at her daughter, and back to Kay. His smile spoke volumes. "Thank you," he mouthed.

Kay raised her shoulders and lowered them with a deep sigh. *God, help us all.*

CHAPTER 15

It was almost noon when the surgeon came to talk to them. The waiting room had filled steadily as the morning wore on. Besides families of other patients, Madge and Agnes had arrived mid-morning with Sadie. Franklin noted Kay's mother hadn't let go of Dana's hand since their first introductory hug.

The doctor motioned them to follow, and Franklin, Wilhelmina, Dana, Sadie, and Kay joined him in a small conference room. "Surgery went reasonably well. Drew is strong and should have no trouble with recovery. Wade, on the other hand... Time will tell. They're both in recovery now. We'll assign them to the same room, but they won't get there for a couple hours, at least." He glanced around, and Franklin became aware of their disheveled appearance. "Take a break," the doctor said. "It's been a long night."

They began to collect their belongings from the waiting room. Wilhelmina insisted she would take Dana to the house where she could shower and nap, saying they'd be back by three or four. Kay said she'd stay. Franklin admired her stamina.

Minutes later, he unlocked the door to his home and stepped aside for his wife and granddaughter to enter.

"I'm going to throw something together in the kitchen," Wilhelmina said. "It's been a while since any of us ate. Dear, would you show Dana to the guest room?"

Franklin lifted Dana's backpack and looked for another suitcase. "This is all you have?"

"I didn't want to take time to check luggage."

He led her up the stairs of their home. The guest room was on the third floor, but on a whim he led her down the hall of the second floor.

He pushed open a door and stood back for her to see.

"Oh, Grandpa, this is beautiful! It's so retro. I wouldn't have imagined Grandmother would decorate like this."

He tried to see the room the way Dana did, but instead was flooded with memories of his daughter Sharon. The peach colored walls complimented her strawberry hair, so similar to Dana's before she turned it blonde. She used to sit at that vanity trying new shades of lipstick and asking what he thought. He remembered when she was little enough to want him to tuck her in. He used to skip pages in her storybook to hurry through it. He wished now he hadn't done that. There was the lava lamp she had begged him for when they were shopping for a birthday present for Wilhelmina.

He nearly jumped when he heard his wife's voice behind them. "This was Sharon's room, Dana. Franklin, I thought you were taking her to the guest room."

"This felt right, dear."

"Don't be silly. This room hasn't been used in years. The guest room has fresh linen." Her hands were on her hips, a bad sign.

Dana had entered the room and was examining the books on the shelves. Franklin lowered his voice. "It's time, Willie. Look at her. Doesn't the room look right with her in it?"

Their granddaughter glanced up from a book she had opened. "This was one of my favorites! Did Sharon like horses?"

Wilhelmina took a deep breath and let it out. "Yes, loved them. She was quite a rider."

"I always wanted my own horse." She returned the book carefully to its shelf. "Maybe when I'm a doctor I'll be able to afford one."

Franklin mouthed to Wilhelmina, "Let go."

Wilhelmina wiped a tear from the corner of one eye. "Enjoy the room, Dana. Sharon would have loved you staying here. We'll eat in ten minutes and then we all should try to sleep before we head back to the hospital."

Franklin closed the door and took his wife in his arms. "Thank you, Willie. You are one beautiful Grandma."

She returned his hug, then stepped back. "Grandmother. I'm more a grandmother than a grandma. Don't you think?"

"Frankly, my dear, to me you are still a teenager!"

She gave him a lopsided smile, but they both were too frightened for light spirits.

Seeing the worry return to her eyes, Franklin assured her, "He'll be all right. They'll both be fine. They have to be."

The words were frighteningly familiar. He'd said the same thing about Tiffany.

#

Kay knew she couldn't leave the hospital, and Madge and Agnes assured her they would help Sadie home. When a nurse realized Kay would stay, she spoke to the receptionist. Kay was shown to the room her two men would share. A recliner sat between the beds, and she sank gratefully into it and almost immediately into sleep.

She roused when her son was rolled in. "Hey, Mom. Knew you'd be here."

She doubted he could have said anything more meaningful. That was what she wanted for her children, to know she would always be there for them. To her, that was love.

"I feel wretched about this, Drew." But he had drifted back to sleep. Kay sank into the recliner, drained of all energy but filled with emotion.

#

Wade woke slowly. His first awareness, after the antiseptic smell, was of a bell near his head. Each time it rang, a woman's voice reminded him to, "Breathe, Mr. Hampton." The third time he heard the dinging, he quipped, "Breathe, Mr. Hampton." A petite blonde nurse came into his view.

"Welcome back, Mr. Hampton. You're in Recovery. You've been in surgery and the anesthetic suppresses your breathing reflex. The bell helps you wake enough to remember to breathe deeply."

"Surgery?"

"Yes, you arrived at the hospital in acute kidney failure. You are recovering from a transplant, thanks to your son."

"Son? I don't have a son."

"Relax, Mr. Hampton. You'll be thinking more clearly soon." She made notes on a chart and bustled away.

Wade turned his head left and right, but could only see curtains. His eyes fought to close. His thoughts jumped, recalling bits and pieces.

The pine scent of the lake cabin.

Kay. Don't leave.

Kidney failure.

Don't tell. Promise me.

Wade surrendered into oblivion.

#

He didn't know how long he had slept before he woke again. "Where am I?"

A disembodied voice answered, "You're in the hospital, Mr. Hampton, recovering from kidney transplant surgery."

The answer made him feel angry, but he didn't remember why.

He slept.

#

When he woke again, he listened to the sounds around him. Beeps, motors, hurrying footsteps. He struggled to orient himself. A hospital. "St. James?"

The now familiar voice answered as it approached. "Yes, you were in the Anaconda hospital. They say you collapsed at your lake cabin and your wife brought you there. They transferred you to us for surgery." The petite blonde came into view and studied something behind him before making notes on her chart.

"My wife is dead."

She nodded and smiled with a look women give children. "Anesthesia does strange things to us. You'll be more yourself soon."

A familiar nausea rolled over him, and Wade dismissed the conversation, more concerned with the state of his stomach.

#

The next time he woke the recovery room was quieter. The nausea had subsided enough to allow him to struggle with his thoughts instead of his stomach. Kay dominated the images that visited him. Kay in her condo, looking so good he wanted to hold her. Kay in his office, stirring his emotions with her unannounced visit. Kay at the funeral.

Tiffany's funeral. Tiffany was gone. Why was Kay there? Kay dragging him? And the smell of forest. Not up to the effort to think clearly, he slept.

#

Kay awoke when Wilhelmina, Franklin, and Dana arrived. She righted the recliner and stood, running her fingers through her hair. Wilhelmina looked perfectly groomed.

Dana glowed. She seemed completely at ease with her companions. Giving Kay a quick kiss on the cheek, she whispered, "How are the patients? Where's Dad?"

"Drew's been asleep. I guess your dad is still in Recovery."

A nurse leaned into the room. "Three visitors, max."

Kay and Wilhelmina exchanged glances. Kay picked up her purse. "I'll take a break. Dana, want to come get something to eat?"

"No thanks, Mom. The Hamptons fed me royally. I want to stay here with Drew."

Kay nodded and left, feeling outcast.

#

Wade dreamed of pine trees rushing past him. He was running, carrying a bundle. He opened it and two babies began to cry. Twins. His twins. He had to protect them from someone with a knife. But Kay blocked his way. He woke with a start.

"Oh good, you're awake." This voice wasn't the blonde's. An older woman in white came into view. "Doc says you can be moved out of Recovery. Your family will be anxious to see you."

Two men lifted Wade from the bed to a gurney. The pain distracted him and he closed his eyes against it. When he opened them, lights on the ceiling rolled past him. The nausea returned. The wheels bumped and the pain surged. He tried to breathe shallowly. A chill swept down his body. The motion stopped and he opened his eyes. Kay kissed his cheek. The rumbling motion started again and he squeezed his eyes tight against his stomach's reaction. When the motion stopped, he dared to open them again.

A young man in the bed next to his waved weakly at him. "Hi Dad. I'm Drew."

His mother and father approached his bed. And a pretty young woman. Sharon? Sharon was dead. Dead like Tiffany.

Wade rolled to the side of the bed away from the stranger and vomited. He didn't remember why, but before slipping back to sleep he knew this was Kay's fault.

CHAPTER 16

Kay dialed the number Drew had given her, but didn't know what to pray the response would be. *Bless Drew's future*, was the best she could ask.

"Twenty-fifth Infantry Division."

"This is Private Drew Collie's mother. May I speak to his commanding officer, please?"

"Yes, Ma'am. I'll connect you."

Kay waited and tried to plan her words. A gruff voice barked, "Sergeant Major Brown."

She introduced herself, then continued, "Sergeant Brown—"

"Sergeant MAJOR Brown, Ma'am."

"I'm sorry. Sergeant Major Brown, my son came home yesterday on emergency leave to see his father who was critically ill."

"Yes, I'm sorry about your husband, Ma'am."

Kay didn't bother to correct him on their relationship but realized letting people assume Wade was her husband could become habit forming. "Sergeant Major, his father needed a kidney transplant. Drew was a match."

"My apologies, Ma'am, but Private Collie must apply for military permission before he can be an organ donor."

"The surgery is over. Drew's leave will need to be extended for recovery time."

"With all due respect, Ma'am, he had no right to make that kind of a decision without the permission of his commanding officer. The Army owns his body."

She couldn't believe her ears. She'd have laughed if she didn't realize the man was dead serious. "I'm afraid the Army owns one less kidney now. What are we going to do about it, Sergeant Major?"

"Please give me the phone number where Private Collie can be reached. I'll send this up the proper channels, but I can't guarantee he won't be discharged."

Kay's stomach tightened and she sobered. "I'll appreciate whatever you can do. Drew hopes to make the Army his life."

She recited the phone number and hung up, dreading the prospect of telling her son about the conversation.

#

When Wade next woke, the room was bright with morning sun. He turned his head to his left and saw that the stranger Drew still slept. Between the two beds, Kay dozed in a recliner. Her presence caused a surge of conflicting emotions. He wanted her. Always had, even while he was married and she was little more than a memory. But she had betrayed him. Not once but twice. Years ago when she disappeared. Yesterday when she broke her promise. He had begged her not to tell their children…

She stirred and opened her eyes. Her face lit when she saw him looking at her. The curve of her lips made him want to stroke her cheek. Then he focused beyond her and saw their sleeping son. How could she have done this? He clenched his fists and turned away from her.

She kept her voice low. "I had to tell them. I couldn't let you die."

He didn't respond.

"I know I promised, but you weren't yourself. You weren't thinking clearly. I needed to calm you down. The promise was the only way I could do that."

"So I finally meet a son I didn't know I had until yesterday, and I can't even walk over and shake his hand."

"But you're alive."

He had no answer for that. He turned back to her. "The girl with hair like Sharon, she's our daughter?"

"Yes, that's Dana. College freshman. Brilliant future doctor. Always an optimist."

He glanced at the other bed and lowered his voice. "And Drew?"

"Drew is a protector, always ready to defend someone. Gets that from his dad who rescued me once."

Wade remembered that night so long ago. And the wedding and short honeymoon that followed. He stopped his thoughts, determined to avoid remembering the painful days that followed. "Is he in college?"

"Army. Enlisted right after high school graduation. He's on leave before being assigned to computer school." Kay's face changed. She had been almost glowing, but the sparkle left her eyes.

"What's wrong?" He could see she vacillated before answering.

She straightened her shoulders. "We aren't sure what this surgery will mean for his military service. There's a chance he'll be discharged. But it was his choice. He decided to do this."

"Why did you tell him? You promised me you wouldn't."

"I'm sorry. I never thought I'd break a promise to you." She lowered her eyes. "He'd never have forgiven me... I'd never have forgiven myself if I didn't give him the choice."

Wade shook his head. "I broke my promise to you years ago and have been paying the price ever since. I swore I'd never break a promise again."

"My mother wouldn't break her wedding vows. You did. In both cases, I paid the price for years. When we make mistakes, often it's the innocent—"

His mother and daughter slipped into the room. Kay rose, hugged Dana, and slipped out without looking back.

Wade sank back against his pillow. For once he'd like to finish a conversation without Kay leaving before he was done.

"Hi, ...Dad." Dana's voice reminded him again of Sharon. Reminded him of the guilt for not being there the night of her car accident.

He reached a hand up and Dana squeezed it. "Hi Dana. Nice to meet you, finally." He hadn't been there for all of his daughter's life either. His sense of regret intensified. How did she feel about him? "I see you're getting to know your grandmother."

Wilhelmina beamed at the title. She had longed for years to be a grandmother. He had wanted to give her that, but Tiffany...

Wilhelmina leaned over and kissed Wade's cheek. Her aroma hung near him when she stood back. *Emeraude*. His gift to her every Christmas since his early teens. Now her eyes were filling as she studied him.

"You gonna share the visitors, Dad?" Both women turned and Dana punched Drew's shoulder. He grabbed the shoulder and groaned, "Oh, my stitches!"

Obviously Dana wasn't too worried. "Sutures, not stitches. Can I see where they really are?" She tugged at his covers, but Drew held them down.

"Pre-med students are so weird. You probably wish you could have been the match. You would have stayed awake to watch."

Dana turned to her father. "I would have helped, you know, if I matched. I wish I could have been the one."

"I asked your mom not to tell either of you. I didn't want you to go through this, especially not knowing me." The meds were making him emotional. It took quick blinking to keep his eyes clear.

"Obviously Mom figured you were delirious." Dana added a lopsided grin to the comment. "I'm glad she did."

Wilhelmina exhaled dramatically. "Thank God she did. She saved your life, Wade, and you should be grateful."

Could being a grandmother have softened his mother? He dodged her rebuke. "So Dana, tell me all about yourself. You too, Drew. We have catching up to do."

#

The surgeon looked worn out when he came in to talk to Wade. "You're one lucky, man. You know that don't you?"

Wade glanced over at Drew. "Thanks to you two, yes."

"And your, uh, Ms. Collie. If she hadn't found you, you wouldn't have made it. Time for some life changes, Mr. Hampton. You've got to take your diabetes seriously."

"My wife's illness overshadowed my own troubles."

"Doctor's orders, now. You must put your needs first, or at least equal with others. This fine young man deserves to have his father around for many more years."

Wade met Drew's eyes. His son nodded.

"Mr. Hampton, you'll be discharged soon, assuming all continues as expected. But you'll need help for a while. I'd prefer you to be under a nurse's care at home, if possible. We could transfer you to a nursing facility if that can't be arranged."

"No, I want to go home. I'll hire a private nurse until I'm back to myself."

"Fine, figure nursing care for at least a couple of weeks."

"Thank you, Doctor."

The doctor left and Drew turned on the television, but Wade's thoughts were captured by the doctor's orders that he put his needs on as high a level as others'. Apart from everyone else's wants, what did he want? He had pushed down his own desires for so long he was surprised at how immediate and sure he was about his preferences. He wanted one particular nurse to share his home. One woman whom he had loved for more than twenty years. But Kay was taking care of her mother and now would have Drew to care for, too. And only weeks had passed since Tiffany's death. It wasn't a reasonable dream…

He considered his son and a hot, bitter anger surged and engulfed the dream. Kay had kept him from knowing his own children all these years. She had broken her promise and jeopardized his son. She was responsible for Drew lying next to him in a hospital.

How could she?

CHAPTER 17

Kay's days passed in a blur. The Hamptons and Dana visited the hospital together. Kay and occasionally Sadie stayed whenever the others weren't there. Often she paused outside the door to listen to Drew chatting excitedly with his father. Wade answered in a weaker but animated voice. The two men in her life were becoming close, but conversation died when she entered the room. She longed to clear the air with Wade, but not in front of their son. Anger radiated from both beds and strained the hours she spent sitting between Wade and Drew. She didn't know how the visits were going for Dana and the Hamptons, but judging from Dana's smiles as they passed each other, her daughter grew fond of Wade.

The Hamptons. Kay had hardly gotten more than moments here and there with her daughter. When she did, Dana chattered about how wonderful her grandparents were. Sadie was feeling left out too, though she seemed to accept it better than Kay.

On the day Drew was to be released, Kay made up the bed in the living room for him so he wouldn't have to maneuver the stairs. Sadie had suggested it and moved her things into the room they had expected Dana to use before she decided to stay with the Hamptons. Kay was touched that her mother would relinquish that connection with her father. Her parents had shared the corner of the living room as their bedroom for all the years Kay had been gone.

She dreaded the task but finally forced herself to call Sacred Heart Hospital in Spokane. She asked for Margaret, her supervisor.

"Kay!" Her boss's voice sounded nasally. "Tell me you're ready to come back. Six weeks without you around has shown us how much we need you! Lousy cold is going through the staff."

"Actually, Margaret, my mother is doing better, but my son had major surgery. I'm afraid I'll need a few more weeks."

The pause on the line caused the hair on Kay's neck to prickle.

"Kay, we can't hold out. We are short-handed as it is and trying to cover your shift has stretched all the nursing staff. We need you back."

"Margaret, I have to take care of my son. He's a kidney donor. He'll need more time to gain his strength back. And my mother still isn't capable of staying on her own."

"I'm sincerely sorry. I hate losing a nurse as capable and caring as you, but I'm going to have to hire a replacement."

She had worked for Sacred Heart since she was eighteen, first as an aide, then as a nurse. She had never turned down a request to fill in a shift. But now, when she needed.... Kay shook away the thought. She knew how it was. The work had to get done. She'd been gone for weeks. Of course they couldn't save her position. Kay struggled to keep her voice steady. "I understand. I appreciate how long you've already waited for me."

Margaret's voice softened. "I'll write a glowing recommendation letter."

Kay murmured her appreciation and hung up. At least she would have time with Drew. They needed a chance to heal their relationship. He'd come around and understand how difficult her decisions had been.

However, when Kay arrived at the hospital, Drew's bed was empty. She turned to Wade, "Where is he?"

"Mother and Dad came early. Drew checked out and went home with them." The anger that had hardened Wade's eyes now held only sympathy.

Kay sat, stunned. After all those years, what she feared most had come true. She began to tremble and wrapped her arms around herself.

"I'm sorry, Kay." He reached a hand to her.

Rather than break down in front of Wade, she turned on him. "Sorry. For what? For abandoning me nineteen years ago? For letting your mother come between us then, or for letting her steal my children now? For marrying Tiffany when I was waiting for you?"

"That's not fair!" His voice was weak, but the anger in it surprised Kay and forced her back under control.

She gentled her tone. "My greatest fear was losing them the way I lost you."

"You left me, remember? I searched. I waited." He turned his head away from her.

Should she push the conversation? Was he strong enough now? He'd better be because she wouldn't hold it in any more.

"I couldn't stay once I saw your signature on the annulment papers," she said.

"I needed to do something to calm my mother. She had lost Sharon and couldn't bear to lose me, too."

"So you let me bear it instead?"

He turned back towards her. "I never meant for it to be over between us. I thought we'd give them some time to grieve, and when they had adjusted to the idea we'd have a big wedding."

This was news to Kay. She paused. "It would have been nice if you'd let me in on your plan."

"I would have if I could have found you."

"Your mother made sure we wouldn't get together."

The frustration in Wade's voice grew. "Why didn't you contact me, tell me where you were?"

"I promised I wouldn't. That was your mother's condition, her bribe." Maybe he hadn't known that, but did it make a difference?

"Why did you take the money? Why didn't you stay? Wasn't I worth more than $20,000?"

It always came back to the money. Did she have to spell it out? "Because of the babies. I needed the money for them. I knew she would take them if she found out about them. Obviously, I was right. She has them both!"

Kay stormed out of the room, determined to never return. Wilhelmina had finally done what Kay feared her whole adult life. She took her children away from her. With Drew already angry and Dana spending all her time with the Hamptons, it wouldn't be long before Wilhelmina turned them against her. Just like she had with Wade.

She drove to the Hampton house and pounded on their door.

Wilhelmina answered. "For heaven's sake, Kay, be quiet. Drew needs his rest."

"I want to see him. You had no right to take him away."

"I had every right. He's my grandson, he's an adult, and he asked us to bring him here."

"I want to see him. Hear it for myself."

Wilhelmina moved in front of Kay. "No. He doesn't want to see you."

"Dana! Drew!" Kay called, but Wilhelmina stepped outside and closed the door behind her.

"Really, Kay, you are making quite a scene. You've had your children for 18 years all to yourself. Can't you share them for a few days? Dana and Franklin left to visit Wade. Drew is asleep. I'll ask him to call you when he wakes up." She turned on her heel and went back into the house, engaging the lock with a decisive click.

Kay stood staring at a welcome sign that camouflaged the Hampton's peep hole. What was she doing raging on their doorstep? How could she have let Wilhelmina bring her to this point? She closed her eyes and forced herself to take several deep breaths.

Only this morning she had worried about how she would care for both her mother and Drew.

Her job! She could call and get it back.

But Sadie wasn't self-sufficient yet. And Drew might change his mind. She needed more time.

#

Kay returned to her mother's house and explained that Drew had chosen to stay with Hamptons. When she saw the disappointment on Sadie's face, she realized she had been focusing only on her own pain. Wilhelmina was right, Kay had enjoyed years with her children, but Sadie had barely gotten to visit with them while they had been in Butte.

"Oh, Mama, I'm sorry. I should have found a way for you to know them."

Her mother patted her hand. "I'm not dead yet, Kay. There'll be time ahead, God willing."

Kay bustled around getting lunch for the two of them. The thought of her mother's death shook her. Two months ago, it wouldn't have made much difference in her life, and she might not have even known about it until she read the Butte paper. Now she realized how deeply she would feel the loss of her mother. She needed to have her near.

She joined her mother at the table for salad. "Mama, what would you think of moving back to Spokane with me soon? I have two bedrooms."

Sadie set down her fork. "Oh heavens, no, Kay. My life, my work, my memories, my friends are all here. I couldn't leave."

So, that settled it. Her mother wouldn't move, but still needed help. She would have to give up her job and trust God to help her find another one. But not yet. Not until Drew recovered.

Drew. If he couldn't be in the military, what would he do?

#

Kay waited, hoping Drew would call, but when the phone rang, she heard Dana. "Mom, I'd like to come over and say goodbye. I'll leave in the morning to get back to school."

"So soon? But yes, of course you need to get back to your studies." Kay could see Sadie, who was dozing in one of the blue chairs, holding Kay's unfinished portrait in her lap. "I wish you had gotten more time with my mother."

"Me, too. But there will be other chances, now that we all have met. Maybe both families will celebrate holidays together."

Kay held her eyes closed, imagining. No, only her daughter could be that much of an optimist. No reason to share her doubts, though. "You never know. But definitely I'll see you for Thanksgiving?"

"Of course. Wouldn't miss it. I'll be over in about ten minutes."

"Wait, Dana?"

"Yes?"

"Tell your brother I love him, all right?

"He loves you, too, Mom. He'll come around."

Kay hung up the phone and moved toward her mother to rescue the portrait that threatened to slip from her lap. Sadie startled awake.

"Sorry, Mama, didn't mean to disturb you. I thought I'd set the portrait down for you."

Sadie straightened and considered the painting. "I love how your father portrayed you." She tilted her head and studied Kay. "You don't have the same vulnerable look in your eyes anymore. You're stronger." She frowned. "Angry some, too."

"Who me?" She laughed but without humor.

"Kay, I've been thinking about the argument you had with Wade this morning." She glanced again at the two dimensional Kay in her lap.

"Anyone would be angry in my place."

"But you left. You tend to not give people a chance to work out their disagreements with you. What makes you run?"

"Mama, all those years that Dad would stomp up the stairs, I used to wish he would leave. Or wished I could. I guess I get scared."

"Of what Wade will do if you stay?"

"Maybe of what I might do. What if the rage Dad felt is part of me?"

Sadie shook her head slowly, then abruptly focused on Kay, concern in her eyes. "Kay, dear, when the twins were little…"

"No, Mama, I never hurt them, even when I was exhausted. There were times I put myself in 'time out,' but I never raised a hand to them."

Sadie's face relaxed. "Then I think you have your answer. You have self-control. I can't imagine you'd ever hurt anyone on purpose."

"Thank you, Mama. I hope you're right."

"Kay, you need to go back to see Wade. Finish a talk with him, even if it's difficult. Stay and don't leave until you've both said all there is to say."

"I'll give it some thought. For now, though, I'm going to put on the tea kettle. Dana's coming over to visit. She'll head back to school tomorrow."

Sadie's grin was contagious. "You see, she's accepted your choices. Drew will too in his own good time."

"How can you be so patient, Mama?" Kay called from the kitchen. "I want to go drag him here by his ears."

"I have lots of practice waiting for loved ones to come home." Sadie's words were soft, but they pierced Kay's heart. Her mother had felt exactly as forlorn as Kay felt now. And had endured it for nineteen years.

Please God, don't let Drew be as stubborn as his mother. Show us both how to forgive.

#

Kay sat with her fingers wrapped around the mug, enjoying the warmth as much from the mug as from watching her daughter and her mother getting to know each other better.

"So you're going to be a doctor?"

"Yes, Grandma. I hear hospitals have been in our family's blood for three generations now."

Sadie quipped, "In our blood… Ground into our knees…"

The other two laughed but Kay flinched. She had always regretted the necessity of her mother scrubbing floors and toilets for a living.

Sadie told Dana stories of the strange things that she had witnessed working in the hospital. Once she had been dusting under a bed when she noticed a diamond ring. The young woman in the bed swore it wasn't hers. She didn't want the handsome man who visited her to know she was engaged. Of course, as soon as he left, the woman complained that Sadie had stolen her ring. Luckily Sadie had turned it in to security as soon as she left the room.

"That didn't beat the time one of the patients asked me to marry him!"

"You're kidding, Grandma." Dana blushed and quickly added, "Not that anyone wouldn't want to marry you, of course."

Sadie laughed. "He was half blind and had left his dentures at home but he liked how hard I worked. Wouldn't mind having shomeone like me around hish kitshen."

Dana giggled.

"There were days I wished I could have taken him up on it, too."

Dana talked of new friends she had met at school and the challenge of sharing a room with a girl who rose at 5 a.m. for crew practice. Kay listened and loved her daughter for the open heart that let her accept an unknown parent and three grandparents into her life so quickly.

The evening flew by and it seemed too soon when Kay reluctantly walked with Dana to the car the Hampton's had loaned their granddaughter. She hadn't thrown on a coat, so she shivered as she waited for Dana to get in and start the engine.

Dana rolled down the window and blew her a kiss. "I wish you hadn't waited so long to share your past with us, Mom. It's been great being able to know our family. They're all wonderful."

"You get along with your Hampton grandparents?" The notion baffled her. They had always seemed the villains in her mind.

"They're super, Mom. Very generous. You should hear all the fundraisers and charities Grandmother works on."

Kay felt an urge to vindicate herself to her daughter. She could tell her how they had destroyed her life with one piece of paper. Stolen her happiness and shattered her dreams. But the innocent love on her daughter's face stopped her. "That's great, Dana. I'm glad you like them."

"And Grandma Sadie's a riot! Too bad you didn't get her sense of humor. You were always working so hard for us."

Kay had never realized she didn't portray much of a light heart. It was true though, she had needed to fight for the welfare of her children. All because of the *generous* Wilhelmina.

She rubbed her hands up and down her arms and then waved as Dana backed out of the driveway. "I'll see you off at the airport tomorrow. Good night. I love you!"

Was it all the Hampton's fault? Her conscience objected. What if she had learned to ask for help? What if, when Wilhelmina had brought the annulment paper she had told her she couldn't sign because she was pregnant and needed Wade beside her? What if she had insisted on talking to Wade before she made such life-changing decisions?

Talking to Wade. She'd take her mother's advice and try one more time.

CHAPTER 18

After Dana's flight left the airport, Kay drove to the hospital. She was about to step into the elevator when Wade's father stepped out. Franklin motioned toward the cafeteria. "May I buy you a cup of coffee? I'd like to talk to you."

Kay considered. Maybe she'd give him a piece of her mind about taking her children away from her.

"Please," he said.

She nodded and they continued together in silence.

When they were settled with their drinks at an isolated table, Kay waited for Franklin to explain why he wanted to see her.

Franklin released a slow breath and stared at his coffee cup. Finally, he pointed to Kay's hand. "You're married."

"No." She wondered where this might lead.

"But you wear a wedding band. May I ask why?"

She considered the ring before answering. "It kept the wolves at bay." It felt right having it back on her hand since bringing Wade into the Anaconda hospital.

"Why didn't you remarry?"

"I'd been too hurt by men."

His look reminded her of his courtroom mastery. He waited to hear the rest of the story.

"You're right. There was more to it than that. I still felt married. Even after the years wore on. I was married for a matter of days, but Wade was my soul mate and my soul didn't pay attention to time."

"Still felt married...." His eyes lost focus and Kay wondered what he was thinking.

When he turned his attention back to her, he assumed the decisive lawyer persona again. "Kay, we owe you an apology. We thought we were doing the right thing. The law allows for annulments in cases where the parties involved might not have been thinking clearly, or were under duress."

This didn't sound like an apology. It sounded like excuses. But Kay only shifted back a bit in her chair. With her mother's admonition to not run from difficult conversations still fresh on her mind, she would hear him out.

"We thought at first that was the case. You were escaping from— shall we say—a less than perfect home life. If it were today, I would be required by law to report your father for my suspicions."

Kay crossed her arms. He didn't have a right to be commenting on her upbringing.

"Then when you accepted Wilhelmina's offer—"

"Bribe."

His face flashed irritation, but he mastered it and shrugged his shoulders. "Yes, I guess it seemed like a bribe. For her it seemed a way to test your commitment. When you took the offer, we thought it proved you married Wade for the wrong reasons."

Kay stood.

He gestured quickly. "Sit, sit, sit. I still owe you that apology, and I'm coming to it."

She eased into her chair, again remembering her mother's advice not to run from conflict.

"We are immeasurably sorry that we drove you away. Now that we have met Drew and Dana, we understand. You took the money for them." He leaned in. "But why did you leave? Why didn't you tell anyone about your pregnancy? You certainly had a right, and you would have been where family could help you. Where *we* could have helped you."

Kay doubted they would have helped, but she tried to answer his questions. "You had been able to take away my marriage. I was afraid a family of lawyers could take custody of my children, too. After all, what did I have here to offer them? To live with a grandfather who…" She swallowed. Years of covering for her father made it hard to break old habits.

She reframed. "It wouldn't have been a happy home to raise a child in. With your money, I was able to go to school and, even though I had to give up my dream of being a doctor, I could become a nurse and support them. The money bought me time."

"I see."

She waited while Franklin sat silently, drumming his fingertips together. She hadn't noticed before how much he had aged.

"You wanted to be a doctor." He didn't look at her.

When medical school became impossible, she had shifted her dream. She nodded, remembering her envy of the students as she left Dana at college. But it was too late.

"That dream will have to be Dana's. For now I'd better start looking for a new nursing job." She stood, feeling he had said what he wanted to. "I appreciate your apology, Franklin."

He rose as she left, but she had the feeling his thoughts had moved far beyond their conversation.

#

Kay checked her watch. There still was time, but she felt emotionally drained so decided to postpone her visit with Wade. She hurried home to make dinner for her mother. When Kay pushed open the back door, she smelled roast beef and onions. Bless those church women, she thought. She glanced into the living room but didn't see her mother. She called up the stairs, "Mom, I'm home. You here?"

"Be down in a minute! Sit. I have a surprise."

Kay sank into one of the blue chairs, enjoying the moment off her feet. "Who started the roast?" she called.

Her mother regally descended the stairs in grand entry fashion. "I did."

"Mom, your sling is gone! Oh! You had a doctor appointment today and I forgot all about it."

Her mom grinned. "Madge took me. Watch this!" She raised her hand shoulder-high and waved.

Kay laughed and waved back. "Looks like you won't need me much longer. You're even cooking now! But it will still be a while before you have the strength to scrub at the hospital. How will you work?"

"Oh, Kay, dear. I've been the housekeeping supervisor for years. I don't scrub anymore. Those days are long gone, thank heavens. I'll be back to writing schedules and ordering cleaning supplies and checking to keep our hospital up to standards. That I can do with one good arm. Plus, in a matter of months I'll be eligible to retire. I might do just that."

"Can you afford to, Mom?"

"I'll be fine, Kay. Your father's painting brought us a nice nest egg. Don't you worry about me."

With surprise, Kay realized her feelings were mixed. With Dana at school, Drew at the Hamptons, and now her mother almost back to normal, Kay wasn't needed by anyone. She felt like a teenager having an identity crisis. All her adult life she had been a nurturer, both at home and at work. Now no family remained to nurture.

The phone rang. Her mother had gone to check the oven, so Kay answered it.

Wilhelmina's grating voice managed to set Kay's nerves on edge, even over the phone. "Kay, Franklin told me about your conversation at the hospital. I'd like to talk to you, too. Could you drop by tomorrow morning?"

Her mother reached up into the cabinet with her right hand and handed plates down to her newly freed left. Visiting Wilhelmina was the last thing she wanted, but she didn't seem to have an excuse not to. "Looks like that won't be a problem."

#

Kay knocked gently on the Hampton's front door, blushing as she remembered last time when she hadn't rapped so civilly. Did she dare hope Drew would consent to seeing her this time?

Wilhelmina opened the door and invited her in, this time to sit at the kitchen table. The atmosphere was so much more informal than the last time Kay was invited, when Wilhelmina asked her to go to Wade's cabin. Rather than the silver teapot and porcelain tea cups her hostess filled two mugs at the stove and brought them to the table, each with a steeping teabag.

"I know you saved Wade's life, Kay," Wilhelmina said. "I want to thank you. When I said you might be the only one who could, I didn't realize how true that would be."

"I went with my own agenda. I wanted to tell Wade about the twins before they arrived. It didn't work out the way I hoped."

Wilhelmina took a slow drink of tea. "Neither did my plans nineteen years ago. I thought I was saving Wade from an unhappy marriage. Instead, I delayed his chance at being a father and mine at being a grandmother. I am truly sorry."

Kay took her time to form her answer. "Mothers do the best they can. Doesn't always work out for the best, but that's all we can do."

Their attention was drawn to slow footsteps. Drew came into the room, his pajamas covered by a robe. "Hey, Mom."

Kay stood. He came to her and they hugged gently, but for a nice amount of time.

"You're right," he said when they disengaged. "Moms do the best they can. I get that. I would have been angrier if you hadn't told me what Dad needed. I couldn't have kept him from dying if you had honored his secret."

She took her chair again and studied her son. "You look good."

"Yeah, Grandma H is taking great care of me. But I miss talking to Dad. I need to recover enough to visit him at the hospital."

"He'll be here before long," Wilhelmina said. "Once he's released he can be right down the hall from you in his old room. You'll have plenty of time to know each other better."

"Wade will be coming here?" Kay hadn't thought that far ahead and realized she was squeezing her mug. She set it down.

"Certainly. He won't be able to take care of himself for quite a while. He can't go back to his house."

Of course. Wilhelmina would have him back. She could afford to be magnanimous with her apologies.

The three visited a bit longer. When Kay stood to go, she asked Drew to come visit his Grandma Sadie as soon as he felt able. He promised he would. Kay left the house, her anger rekindled.

The sunshine that dazzled her eyes against the snow an hour ago had given way to heavy clouds. She hugged her coat closer and wished she were back in Spokane where she never regretted avoiding the Montana winters. Kay started to drive home but found herself headed for the hospital. She felt more at ease in hospitals than she did even now at her mom's house. Memories still occasionally stalked her in the house when she least expected them.

She peeked into Wade's room and was relieved to find him alone. Did his eyes seem to brighten when he saw her? Or was he simply happy to have any company? Days stretched long for patients, she knew.

"Mind if I come in?"

"Not at all."

"I came from your mom's. Had a quick visit with Drew. He doesn't seem angry with me anymore."

"That's good."

An uncomfortable pause caused Kay to wonder whether it was too much to hope Wade might make the progress toward forgiveness that her son had.

"Your hair, you look great."

"Thanks to Francie." She scrunched her hair with one hand, enjoying its softness.

She tried to keep her voice light. "Your mom's looking forward to having you stay with her while you recuperate."

"She's assuming I'll go there?"

"You won't be up to being alone for a while."

"When do you have to return to Spokane? The hospital must be anxious to have you back." He wasn't meeting her eyes.

"I'm not… They had to… They let me go. Couldn't blame them. I've been gone seven weeks. Hospitals can't run short staffed for long."

"I'm sorry." Wade's eyebrows tented. "How's your mom?"

Kay exhaled and sat in the visitor's chair. "She's better. Even got her sling off yesterday. She cooked a roast to celebrate. I lifted it out of the oven, but she'll be self-sufficient soon." She looked at Wade and saw her best friend from high school. Long before they ran away together, he was the one who let her pour out her heart and tell him things she didn't admit to anyone else. Her heart overflowed now, and she spoke to him because he was the one she had always turned to before. "I'm going to miss her. It's been great to reconcile. Great to feel needed."

Perhaps he shared her reminiscence. He reached out and took Kay's hand, but then his eyes darkened and his angry scowl returned. "You have the wedding ring on. You took it off for a while but it's back on again."

Kay touched the gold band. She had left it on since showing it to the doctor, not thinking of how Wade or his family would react.

"I bought it right after I left home. I didn't want to look pregnant and unmarried."

The light returned to his eyes. "So you've worn it all these years? There hasn't been anyone else?"

Kay smiled and shook her head.

"I understand now why you didn't tell me about the twins. But every fiber of my body wishes you hadn't left Butte. Hadn't kept them a secret. You were wrong—"

Kay stood, but Wade's hand stopped her and Sadie's advice not to run held her in place.

Wade hurried on, "—but I was wrong too, to sign the annulment. I was wrong to let my parents do what they did. I'm not going to let anyone make my decisions for me every again."

"You could come take care of me. You could be my nurse." His grin made her suspect what scenario entertained his thoughts.

She drew her hand away. "Doesn't sound exactly appropriate."

"Why not?"

"Dual relationship. Nurses shouldn't work for someone they are emotionally—"

"Are you?"

Kay turned away. "I know you had to let go to be a good husband to Tiffany, but your marriage devastated me. And you, it's too soon since she died for you to be thinking clearly."

Wade focused on picking fuzz off his blanket. "I should have waited for you. It wasn't fair to Tiffany. I couldn't give her my whole heart because you still had a piece of it with you. I didn't know where to look for it."

Kay searched his eyes and her own heart. "Can we put the pain behind us? Is it possible to let go of our wounds?"

He reclaimed Kay's hand and brought it tenderly to his lips. "I've always loved you. Come home and be my nurse."

His kiss sent warmth from her hand to her heart. Kay's eyes welled. She wanted to say yes. She wanted Wade to need her. But the town would talk if she agreed to care for him. Her children, her mother, even his parents deserved better than that.

"I love you, Wade. But you're a new widower. You need time to know you aren't reacting out of grief. I don't want to be a rebound. I couldn't bear to lose you again."

CHAPTER 19

Kay struggled to sleep. Late into the night her cautious mind tried to corral run-away hope.

The next day Sadie took a message from a Spokane phone call while Kay was in the shower.

She dialed the familiar number. "Hi, Margaret, this is Kay, returning your call."

"Kay, have you ever taken the MCAT?"

"No, why?"

"I think you'd better sign up for it. I've got a letter on my desk. A lawyer is representing a client who says your nursing brought blessings to their life. The person wants to sponsor you through med school."

Kay's hands became so sweaty that she almost dropped the receiver. "Who?" She ran a list of possible patients through her mind but couldn't think of any who were wealthy enough or whom she felt she impressed enough for such a gift.

"Anonymous. Letter doesn't say. But MCATs are coming up next week and if you have any desire to ever be a doctor, now's the time to sign up for the admission exam."

Kay could feel herself grinning. Maybe now was the time. Her children were adults. Her mother was healing. Drew seemed to be recovering from giving Wade the kidney.

Wade. Her racing heart came to a standstill and her stomach felt like it dropped.

"When do I need to register? Do I have any time to consider this?"

"Not much. Deadline is Monday for Saturday's test."

It was Friday. She'd need to return to Spokane right away.

"What's wrong, Kay? I thought you always dreamed of being a

doctor. This person is offering to pay tuition, books, even a monthly stipend to get you through."

"So much has changed so fast. This is a huge decision." She dried one palm and then the other on her pants leg, passing the phone back and forth.

"Write down this 800 number. You should call and talk to the lawyer. Ask for Jack Gorman, the letter says."

"Where's it mailed from, maybe that's a hint."

Kay heard rustling and pictured May turning the envelope over. "New York. And the law firm address is New York, too."

"I don't know anyone in New York."

"Obviously your mystery patient does."

#

Kay told her mother the exciting news. Sadie smiled but the light didn't reach her eyes. "When and where would you have to go?"

Again Kay's heart stopped short. She had been gathering her coat and purse, planning to share her news with her high school love, the best friend who could help her consider all the implications. But here was the first of implications and complications. Where would she study? Now that Butte had become a part of her life again, distance mattered. The nearest medical school, University of Washington in Seattle, was more than 600 miles away. Oregon Health and Science University in Portland was worse at 700 miles. How far to South Dakota's Sanford School of Medicine? And would she be accepted at one of those, or need to travel farther?

Dana was studying in Seattle. Who knew where Drew would stay and for how long? Brenda, such a dear friend in Spokane, how often could she see her with this life change? And her mother. How many more years would Sadie be around to enjoy time together?

The phrase, "Be careful what you wish for," came to mind. She had always wanted to be a doctor. She loved nursing, but it hadn't been her dream. Doctoring was. Medical school, choosing a specialty, or maybe setting up a general practice.

She had allowed herself to envision being Wade's wife, though it was too early to assume that would work out. They would need time for him to grieve, time to be together, and time to be sure that finally no one could keep them apart.

She dropped into one of the blue chairs. "Mom, if I start med school, there's no way Wade and I could have a second chance." Saying the words aloud and the sorrow that accompanied them forced Kay to admit how much she wanted that second chance.

Sadie sat in the chair next to Kay's and rested her hand on Kay's arm. "You gave up both those dreams so long ago. Doesn't seem right that you have to choose between them now. There must be a way."

Kay inhaled and shrugged her shoulders.

Sadie leaned forward. "Go, talk to Wade. See how he reacts. Maybe you'll figure out which you want more. I'll pray for your insight."

"Thanks, Mama." She sat up with a start. "You don't suppose he's at the bottom of this, do you?" She shrank from the thought that he might be trying to send her away. Or would he be attempting to fill her heart's desire?

"Only one way to find out. Go."

Kay stood and grabbed her coat on the way to the car, her thoughts and her emotions feeling like they were churning inside a cement mixer. An idea would rise and with it her hopes, then thump, her feelings would drop back into the slurry of loss.

When she arrived at the hospital, she had come no closer to organizing thoughts or feelings. She peeked into Wade's room and found two strangers looking back at her quizzically. "Oh, I'm sorry," she said. "I was looking for Wade Hampton."

A nurse, the little blonde speedball, passed and threw back over her shoulder, "Discharged a couple hours ago."

Kay could have cried. How could she talk to Wade in Wilhelmina's house? The woman had been treating her civilly lately, but that could change at any moment. Especially if she knew that Wade had asked her to be his nurse so that he wouldn't be under his mother's control. She sat in her car a moment and then took out her cell phone.

"Wilhelmina, I hear Wade was released from the hospital."

"Yes, and he's being stubborn. Hired a nurse and moved back home when I could have helped him right here." Wilhelmina's voice faded as she must have turned to Drew. "I'm not a bad nurse, am I, Drew? He would have been fine here."

Kay heard her son's muffled voice, and obviously he satisfied Wilhelmina.

"There, see, he should have come home. It would have given him a chance to spend more time with Drew."

"Wilhelmina, I'd like to talk to Wade about something. Could you give me his address?"

"It's that big blue house, Victorian style, on the corner of Sixth and Copper Road. You know the area?"

"Well enough, thanks. Could I talk to Drew?"

Kay listened to the phone be passed, and Wilhelmina's, "I don't know why he has to be so independent," drifted away.

The man is thirty-seven years old, Kay thought.

"Hey, Mom. She's going to freak when I tell her I want to come spend some time with you and Grandma Sadie. Is that okay?"

Kay grinned. "How soon can I come pick you up?"

"Let's say tomorrow. I think she's had enough rejection today."

"Ok, give me a call and I'll come. How are you feeling?"

"Better each day. Hey, Sergeant Major called. No discharge. Since I'm scheduled for classes they figure I'll do fine recovering before I need to be ready for anything strenuous. You know, like computer crashes or network viruses."

Kay could hear the happiness in Drew's voice. He was going to follow his dream.

So was she, if only she knew which one.

#

Kay drove to Copper Road and parked near the corner of Sixth. She gazed at the only blue house on the four corners. She had always admired these beautiful Victorian homes with cone-roofed turrets. The front porch wrapped around the curve of the turret and white rocking chairs matched the white gingerbread trim. He couldn't have chosen a more perfect match to her dream home if he had asked her to design it. She pictured herself living there but stopped and felt her cheeks burn. This had been Tiffany's house.

Kay rang the lit doorbell and heard a deep chime from within. Through the leaded glass sidelight windows that framed the door, she could see an older woman approach, and Kay tensed when she thought a cigarette dangled from the woman's lips. She restrained a laugh, however, when the woman opened the door and took a lollipop out of her mouth to speak. "Can I help you?"

"I'm looking for Wade Hampton. Do I have the right house?"

"Yes, poor man. Lost his wife and then nearly died himself. She pointed the lollipop at Kay. "You're a friend?"

"I'm Kay Collie. Yes, a friend." She stumbled over the word. But what could she say? His children are mine? I'm his first wife? Ex-wife? She settled on, "I'm the mother of his kidney donor." Coward.

"I'm Nancy. I'll tell him you're here. He's in the guest room, not fit for stairs yet." She disappeared down a hallway and Kay waited by the door.

"Kay!" she heard him call. "Come in!"

She followed the voice and entered a simple but cheery room, painted yellow. Wade sat propped with pillows in a bed beneath a quilt of browns, blues, and yellows that she figured Sadie would have loved to study. He set down a Bible he'd been reading, and she gave thanks for God's handiwork in both their lives.

"Good to see you, Kay."

"You escaped the world of bedpans and IVs."

The nurse brought a chair closer to the bed and then left the room.

Kay sat. "I like your nurse. At first I was afraid she was a smoker until I saw it was a sucker stick."

"Nancy says she used to smoke three packs a day. Now she uses sugarless suckers to get by. I like her, too." He lowered his voice. "Even if she was my second choice."

"Is she taking good care of you?" Kay surveyed the room and noted a filled water glass and a little bell on Wade's nightstand.

"So far, so good. We have only been here a couple hours. And one of those hours was taken up by my mother's temper tantrum." He gave Kay a sheepish grin.

"She likes having you around. Anyone would." Kay felt her cheeks warm at her words.

"She likes being in charge. You know, nearly dying and then having ten days in the hospital to think has given me a new perspective."

Kay sat in the chair near the bed. From this angle she could see that a mantle of snow topped the mountain range that bordered Butte on the east. She dipped lower and could make out the ridge-top Madonna statue built by the townspeople to commemorate motherhood and, most people said, Jesus' mother Mary. "Nice perspective here, too."

"Yeah, kind of ironic that even here a mother is watching me. But that one I find comforting."

Kay nodded. "Wilhelmina's been great with Drew. As much as I hated the idea when he moved in with her, it has probably been good for them both. But if she's as hurt as I was when my son chose not to recuperate with me, I can imagine the tantrum wasn't pretty."

"Always before, I followed my dad's lead. In the courtroom he can dominate anyone, but at home he lets her have her way. She's so good at organizing and leading—every fundraiser she takes on doubles the profit from the previous year—it's easier to go with the flow and do what she wants. It usually turns out for the best." Wade met Kay's eyes and he paled. "But when it goes bad, it can go very bad. Like it did for us."

Kay took comfort in his words and reached to hold his hand. He brushed her knuckles with his thumb and seemed lost in thought.

"So, what's your new perspective on your mom?" she asked.

"More on me, actually. I've lived my life trying to be a peacemaker.

I love helping people get along. Started way back in my childhood. Sharon and Mother were too alike, I think. Flint and steel when they disagreed. I became the go-between who blew out the little flames before they spread."

Wade looked at a point beyond Kay. "I often wonder if I'd been home the night of Sharon's car accident if I might have prevented it. They said she sped off after a huge argument with Mom...."

He focused back on Kay. "I felt guilty about being with you. That's part of why I didn't call you in the weeks before she died. I still regret that."

Kay imagined carrying guilt for his sister's death around for all these years. She had experienced her own heavy load of assumed blame every time her father raged against her or her mother. She told Wade what she tried to believe herself. "You weren't responsible for what they did, or for what happened."

"That's part of what I considered for the past week in the hospital. I'm a peacemaker, but from now on, I'll do it from a stance of strength, rather than weakness. There's a difference between being kind and being appeasing."

"That's why you're here in your own home."

The determined expression on Wade's face made Kay beam her approval.

He held her hand with both of his. "She won't come between us again, Kay. I promise you that."

The thought of something separating her from Wade brought tears to her eyes and reminded her why she had visited.

"Wade, I want to talk to you about something that has come up."

Wade gripped her hand a little tighter. She squeezed his before she drew her hand away and told him about the New York law firm's letter and the mysterious benefactor who had offered to pay her way through medical school. His face registered a volley of emotions.

"Kay, that's wonderful! Your dream, what you always wanted." And then, "But medical schools are so far away." His forehead wrinkled. "With the twins gone, it's an opportune time." The furrows relaxed and he produced a brave smile. "I'm happy for you and sad for me."

"I had to talk to you about this. I thought maybe you were the secret donor."

He shook his head slowly.

"So you think I should do it?" She didn't know how she wanted him to answer.

"Kay, I built this house with you in mind. You must have guessed that. Turrets aren't your everyday house feature."

He reached out and the warmth of his hand on her arm made her mind wander. His words drew her attention back.

"In the last few days you've renewed my hope that you'd live in it someday. But you're right that we need time. I want to beg you to stay in Butte and give us that time, but that would be selfish. I wish I were the one giving you your heart's desire." He let his hand fall from her arm back to the bed. "You can't turn it down."

Kay felt a tear escape from her eye and trail down her cheek. Would they always be plagued with disastrous timing?

"It's not a sure thing. I have to get through the MCATs and even then I might not be accepted anywhere."

"We both know you'll ace it."

"I should leave tomorrow to go back to Spokane to cram." She studied the floor as if it held the answers.

"So soon? Couldn't you study here?" Wade sounded young and vulnerable.

"My books and notes are there. And the medical library..."

"After the test, could you come back here until a decision is made?"

He wanted her with him. For all those years of separation, she dreamed of him wanting her again, loving her, and being her husband. She could stay, work as a nurse, take the time they needed for a solid beginning, not built out of grief or nostalgia, but of choice, love, and commitment. She desperately longed to remain here. But what would she be giving up?

"If I stayed, even for a little while until I'm accepted, I know I wouldn't be able to leave you again." She wiped away the tear trail. It was cruel to have to make such a choice. She wanted to slide next to Wade and lay her head on his shoulder. They had only shared two nights together in one bed, but she still remembered exactly how his skin had felt against hers, and she longed to feel his warmth again.

"I'm only licensed to practice law in Montana."

"I know you can't pick up and follow me wherever I'm accepted. You're established here; I understand that."

"It will be years before you're finished and can set up your own practice."

God seemed to be closing this door and opening another.

She stood, trying to act resolute. "And these weeks, these last couple days, they aren't enough to get us through the wait. We've been apart too long. Your heart isn't healed enough to give away yet. Pour yourself into healing body and soul, Wade. We'll still see each other occasionally. The twins will make sure of that, what with parent weekends and graduation and whatever events the Army has."

She leaned to gently hug him goodbye. He held her tighter when she pulled to leave. His arms made her feel secure and she wanted to hide within his protection. A sob escaped from her chest, and he released his hold.

"I love you enough to let you go," he said with a husky voice.

CHAPTER 20

After Kay left, Wade calmed himself before he telephoned his father.

"Dad, I'd like to talk to you. Could you come over to the house?"

"I've got a three o'clock meeting, but I can make it over for about a half hour. Glad to be settled back at home?"

"Yes. See you soon." Wade felt bone tired. The move from the hospital had drained most of his energy. The emotional visit from Kay sapped any that was left. When Nancy came in to check on him, she was not happy to hear his father was on his way. She insisted Wade lie flat and rest until his arrival. The pillow called him to let go and sleep, but he resisted. He needed to gather his wits for this talk.

When Franklin arrived, Nancy showed him to the guestroom but admonished him, waving the lollipop at him, "Mr. Wade is plumb tuckered. He needs to sleep soon."

Franklin ducked his head down into his shoulders as she left and grinned at Wade. "Reminds me a bit of your mother. She's as mad about you moving home as a judge who's slammed his gavel and declared contempt of court. I'll let her know you're in good hands."

"Dad, do you have a friend that works with the Kinney law firm in New York City?

"Jack Gorman. Why?"

"You tell me."

"Son, I don't know what you are talking about."

"They are representing someone who offered to put Kay through med school. Dad, if this is your way to separate us again--"

"I haven't had contact with Jack in years. I wouldn't do that to you again, I swear. I've never felt right about my part in what happened.

Now, knowing about the twins, I'd love to see you two back together."

Wade watched his father's face carefully. He had studied him for years in court and could notice the slightest of expression changes. He knew some of the intricate thought processes they betrayed.

He relaxed. His father was telling the truth, he was certain.

"I'll tell you what. I'll give Jack a call and see if I can learn anything."

"I'd appreciate it, Dad. Now I'd better rest so I can get back to work before you fire me for slacking off."

Franklin stood to go but then turned. "Is Kay leaving?"

"Tomorrow."

"I'm sorry."

Wade didn't trust himself to respond. He simply nodded.

#

The next morning, Sadie's goodbye-hug nearly started Kay's tears flowing again. They promised to spend Thanksgiving together, though they hadn't decided whether it would be in Butte or Spokane. Then with a final wave, she backed the car out of the driveway and onto the street.

At least Kay wouldn't be making the long drive alone. Drew had decided to ride with her to Spokane and catch an early flight Sunday morning to Georgia, to begin his computer training.

She picked up her son at the Hamptons' home. Drew's mood was as high as hers was low, but she tried to rise above her misery for his sake. He was off to fulfill his dream and treasured it doubly because he thought he had lost it. She followed a dream, too, but devoid of most of its charm due to the sacrifice it demanded.

She drove toward Wade's house knowing she couldn't say goodbye to him again, but Drew wanted to see him one more time before they left. Where weeks ago she had only noticed Butte's rundown buildings, now she noticed the pride people had taken in many others. A woman who swept her walkway with quick strokes glanced up at the passing car and smiled. On another block, two elderly men laughed together at some unheard joke. Wade's next-door neighbor waved as Kay parked in front of his house. Now, minutes away from leaving Butte, Kay realized she would miss the small-town warmth of her community.

She waited in the car while her son disappeared into her dream home.

#

From his position in the living room recliner, Wade watched Kay's car and strained for a view of her. He prayed she would change her mind, but his hope sank when he realized Drew alone would visit.

Nancy answered the door and showed Drew into the living room. He whistled as he entered. "Nice place, Dad."

"Thanks." Wade adjusted the recliner to vertical and indicated a chair near him. "How's your mom?"

"Sad. I thought she'd be more excited about becoming a doctor."

Wade knew he needed to change the topic. The pain medication loosened more emotions than he could fight in front of Drew. "You feeling okay? Healing all right?"

"Yeah, I'm good. Psyched to be able to stay in the service."

"I'm glad that worked out. I was afraid I'd ruined your life plans."

He suddenly couldn't look his son in the eye. Not only because of the surgery. "Drew, I swear if I had known about you and Dana I would have been there for you."

"I believe you, Dad. I don't quite understand why Mom didn't tell you, but I know you would have."

"When I think of the years we missed…. Don't hold it against her, though. She was afraid of my parents and of what they might do. She had her reasons. But they're good people, too. Anyone can do strange things when they're protecting their kids."

Drew cocked an eyebrow. "Like making Mom promise not to tell us you needed a transplant?"

Wade laughed and felt the heat rise up his neck and face. "Like that, yes."

He stood up and held out his arms. Drew rose and bear-hugged his father.

Wade gazed into his son's eyes. "Thank you, Drew, for saving my life. I'm so proud of you. Your service to our country, the fine young man you've become, your love for your mother…"

Drew stepped back. "You love her, too, don't you?"

Wade nodded slowly. "I always have. I still do." For the first time, he realized it was a blessing Tiffany didn't live to know about Kay's return.

"None of my business, probably, but why aren't you two getting back together?"

Wade saw in Drew's face a hint of what his son looked like as a child. "I couldn't stand in the way of your mom's chance at being a doctor. Once before, I kept her from becoming one. I can't again."

Drew scowled, but then offered his hand. The men shook hands and then leaned close for two quick pats on the back. Without further eye contact, Drew left.

Wade kept watch out the window unsuccessfully willing the car not to leave sight.

He wandered in his house until Nancy stopped his pacing by insisting he nap. His body felt weak with exhaustion but he couldn't sleep. His heart was driving farther and farther away.

#

Kay had hoped to catch a glimpse of Wade when Drew came out of the house. How many times now had she kept her gaze on a door, hoping he would come through it to stop her from leaving? She chastised herself. This was her decision. Besides, seeing him would have made it nearly impossible to go.

"Your dad all right?" she asked.

"He loves you, Mom. He doesn't want you to leave. You sure you have to?"

She nodded. But she wasn't sure. She was trying to follow God's leading, but her heart fought her head.

She glanced over at Drew. "Still feel awkward, getting to know your dad?"

"Kinda weird, but I'm glad it finally happened. I can head back to the service feeling more whole." He chuckled. "Even though there's less of me now."

"I'm sorry, Drew. I should have told you long ago. Shared custody somehow."

"No sense thinking about that, Mom. We can't change what's behind us."

"You and Dana deserved a dad."

"We have one now."

While Drew settled into listening to music through his headphones, Kay considered her decision. She would take the MCATs and hope to find work in Spokane until she was accepted and could move to the location of the medical school. Surely this had to be God's will. Think of how many people she could help as a doctor. And wasn't that what she was called to do? To minister with her gifts to God's world? She had been attending to people who needed her ever since she started volunteering as a candy striper in the Butte hospital. Caring, not only for her patients, but her children, and then her mother. She had a gift for nurturing and should use it for others.

So, if God demand she forego a life with Wade, she'd do it. Everyone is asked to surrender. Sacrifice is part of love. Sadie had always said the two walk hand in hand.

But then, why did God send her to Butte? Surely, it was He who announced His call through the Bible passage that unnerved her after Wade arrived. She said God would need to send her own personal angel to get her to go home. She realized He had done exactly that, and she felt almost as if God were laughing at her childish pronouncement. Why Wade? God could have found another way to let her know her parents needed her. Why did He send Wade and then expect Kay to tear herself away from him a second time? Maybe to save his life?

God must be behind this offer of medical school. Who else could have inspired someone to pay her way? The timing of the offer convinced her that God wanted her to leave Wade and be a doctor. She would trust Him to lead her through the pain.

Or show me if I'm on the wrong path. I want to do Your will, even though right now I'd much rather turn this car around.

She wished God would send the same angel He sent before to tell her what to do.

#

When Kay unlocked the door to her condo, the air felt stale and slightly damp from Spokane rains. When she noticed Wade's handkerchief still protecting the coffee table from the glass of water he had offered her, loneliness engulfed her. She grabbed the glass and took it to the dishwasher. The handkerchief she slipped into her pocket, a reminder of Wade's thoughtfulness that she would keep forever.

Drew stood in the living room looking around. He hadn't been home for several months and she knew the rooms would seem empty to him. Not only were his belongings gone, but his sister's, too.

Kay watched him notice the pictures were missing. "The first night I slept here alone I was so miserable I brought every picture of you two into my bedroom."

He leaned into her room and laughed at her arrangement of photos all facing the twin bed.

Kay rested her head on Drew's shoulder and realized he stood as tall as his father now. At the thought of Wade, restlessness grew inside her. "Let's drop our things and go out for dinner. We'll find a nice place. Celebrate your recovery and career."

She would miss her son and fear for him, but she owed it to him to send him off without the burden of worry about her. She put on a bright smile that she knew probably gave her away, but he squared his shoulders and raised an open hand.

"To our new adventures!"

Kay did likewise to give him a high five. "New adventures!" But her heart didn't sing at the thought of being a doctor like it had when she was young.

The next morning she and Drew left the condo early. Both were quiet on the ride and at the airport, alone with their thoughts. When time to join the security screening line, Drew wrapped his arms around her awkwardly. "Take care of yourself, Mom, and don't obsess. I'll be fine."

She looked up to touch his soul with her eyes. "God will be watching over both of us. I'm counting on Him."

Drew nodded and turned to go, but she stopped him with a hand on his arm. "I'm grateful the surgery didn't ruin your career."

He shrugged. "I would have found a way to make it work. I love the military life. No way would I let anyone come between me and what I love."

His words shot through Kay's soul and continued to echo in her mind. She needed her son's courage and drive. She had backed down countless times to her father and then to Wilhelmina. Once and for all, she decided never to back down out of fear again. She'd fight for what she loved. But was that Wade, or a career as a doctor?

They hugged one more time and then he took his place in line.

She stayed until she could no longer see his green-fatigued back as he turned into his concourse. Then she hurried to the ladies' room and locked herself in a stall, weeping over too many partings in her life. How could she survive being alone?

Finally she washed her face and forced herself to breathe smoothly again. On the way to her car, deep gulps of fresh air helped her steady her voice enough to call Brenda, who should be arriving home from church.

"Can I come over?"

"You're home! Come here? ... Of course! I'll put on a pot of tea and you can tell me all about it."

Thank God for dear friends. In her mind, she heard Brenda's voice from one of their scripture studies together, *"Give thanks in all circumstances, for this is God's will for you..."*

She bowed her head before starting her car. "God, I'll try to be thankful. It's easy to be grateful for my children, for Brenda, for a chance to be a doctor. Thank You for bringing my mother back into my life. And Wade. Thank you for bringing him back, too.

"I'm not feeling the least bit thankful that Wade and I are apart again, but You said to be thankful in all circumstances, so I'll try. Please give me the strength to focus on the many people I could help as a doctor, instead of on him. Keep healing him. Watch over our children. Keep me on the path You choose for me."

Feeling only slightly better, she cheered herself by anticipating a good catch-up visit with Brenda. Strange as it seemed, Kay had never been inside Brenda's home. She had picked her up on occasion at the door, but never seen beyond the entry hall. Her own fault, she supposed. Looking back, she could now see how determined she'd been to avoid indebtedness to anyone. Brenda always visited at Kay's home, or for a quick cup of tea at a café.

When she arrived and melted into Brenda's exuberant hug, she had to force herself not to weep on her friend's shoulder. As she stepped back, she caught sight of the dining room table, completely covered with teacups and saucers.

"What in the world?"

Brenda followed her gaze. "Oh, my Jubilee Party favors. I'm going to fill them with teabags and chocolates for the ladies to take home."

"I'd forgotten about your party. How are plans going?"

"I can finally set the date now that you're home!"

Brenda's infectious enthusiasm soon caught Kay up in her friend's tribute to the influential women in her life and she enjoyed a blessed hour of distraction. But on the drive back to the empty condo her thoughts turned to the women God had blessed her with during her time in Butte: Sadie, Francie, her own Dana, and yes, even Madge. She missed them all. She loved them.

It was time to fight for what she loved.

CHAPTER 21

Early on Monday morning at his law office, Franklin called the Kinney law firm and asked to talk to Jack Gorman. He knew he needed to circumvent the lawyer/client privilege carefully.

"Jack, it's been a long time!"

"Good to talk to you, Frankie. Are the backwoods of Montana still holding you back? I'll put a good word in for you when you're ready to move to the big leagues."

Franklin remembered now why he hadn't talked to Jack for years. The man rankled his nerves. But he needed information, so he laughed good naturedly. "No, Jack, I'll leave the big pond to you. I wanted to call and thank you for handling that little matter for us."

"Oh, Wilhelmina told you. I'm glad. Didn't like the thought that I might be going behind your back."

So, it was true. She had done this without even running it by him first. The woman was a master manipulator and he'd had enough of it. Hadn't she done ample damage already? But he had to be certain. "Of course. Miss Collie deserves all the help we can give her."

"That's one lucky nurse, if you ask me. Med school doesn't come cheap. You must not be faring too badly defending cowboys."

"Drop by if you're ever on God's side of the Rockies, Jack."

He leaned back in his leather chair after he'd hung up and considered how to handle Wilhelmina. Wade was right to stand up to her and insist on returning to his house. High time Franklin stood up and had more of a say in his own home.

He glanced at the door to his office. He had closed it, as he often did for privacy during his phone calls. Mary wouldn't enter without knocking. He drew open his top left drawer and lifted out the divider tray that held pens, pencils, letter openers, and miscellaneous clips. With his forefinger and thumb, he pulled a yellowed document from underneath and grimaced at the sight of it. It bore witness to the one time in his career that he had acted without integrity. Sure, there were other times that stretched into gray areas. Lawyers lived in the grey areas of life. But this document crossed the line and could cost him his reputation.

It had been Wilhelmina's idea, of course. But he couldn't say he had been innocent in the affair. He knew the implications. Over the years whenever he looked back and shook his head at his own folly, he had excused himself. He'd been grieving, after all. Why, the very day he drew up this document he had buried his only daughter. But had this paper been part of burying his soul with her?

He had known even then it might result in the very opposite of what he intended. It had succeeded in keeping his son close, rather than losing him to his impetuous elopement, but ever since, Franklin feared it could mean losing him for good if he found out. When he found out. Family secrets don't remain hidden. This one had lasted years, but since seeing Kay Collie at his daughter-in-law's funeral, he'd known their luck wouldn't last.

He was near retirement age. He could weather the storm of reaction if the truth became public, but he couldn't bear to think of hurting his son's reputation, or losing his son's respect.

Still, some considerations were more important than how his son felt about him. His son's happiness, for one. Ethics, for another. Doing the right thing, like he wished he had done years ago. He returned the paper to the drawer, then stood, decided. He would talk to Wilhelmina.

Normally he would have waited for the right time to confront his wife, but he was determined to get this over with as quickly as possible. It made it easier that Drew had moved out. He would miss that boy, though. He was going to be a fine young man.

He found Wilhelmina in the kitchen cleaning out a cabinet. Franklin stopped her with a hand on her arm. "Dear, I need to talk to you about something."

Wilhelmina frowned at him, but followed him to sit at the table.

"I talked to Jack Gorman today." He watched her blanch. "Thanked him for helping us with the anonymous offer to help Kay."

She sat back and her voice came hushed. "How did you know?"

"Wade assumed I arranged it when Kay told him about the letter from New York."

Wilhelmina stared at her lap. While she painstakingly brushed imaginary crumbs from her skirt, he waited. Witnesses often divulged the information he needed if he sat quietly.

Finally she met his gaze. "It's gone all wrong."

"All wrong? Seems you've gotten exactly what you wanted. Kay has left. You've broken them up again. It will cost us more than last time, of course. And I don't mean the money."

Wilhelmina's surprise at Franklin's words showed clearly on her face.

"I swear, Franklin, I was trying to do a good thing. When you came home that night and told me about talking to Kay and how what we did kept her from her dream of being a doctor... She saved Wade's life. And I realized that it was my fault she kept our grandchildren from knowing us. I simply had to do something. I wanted to make it up to her."

Franklin studied her closely. When confident, she lifted her chin like a defiant child. At the moment, her chin almost rested on her chest and her eyes were downcast.

"Last time, of course I maneuvered to keep them apart. This time, I was trying to give her a gift."

"If that's the case, why didn't you talk to me about it? Why all the secrecy?"

"You weren't exactly supportive of my last dream."

"Your adoption plan? Willie, you know that isn't why you didn't tell me."

"I knew you'd suspect my motives." Her chin raised. "I obviously was right. I admit I didn't like Kay. Her family background is certainly not ideal. And she didn't fight for Wade like I would have fought for you. She couldn't have loved him."

"She let go of him for her children's sakes. She's every bit the mama bear you always were."

Wilhelmina's eyes registered Franklin's point. She stood. "God help anyone who would force me to choose between you and my children."

Franklin gentled his voice. "Which is precisely what we did to her. We made her choose between two loves. And now, this misguided attempt of yours to control her life is doing it again. Wilhelmina, for some reason I don't always understand, I love you. I have since law school. I've kept the peace in this house by letting you have your way, even when I shouldn't have. But I will not sit by and allow you to ruin our son's happiness again."

In a shift that Franklin would have thought strategic if not for the vulnerability in her voice, Wilhelmina asked, "Why do you suppose Wade stayed with Tiffany all these years?"

"He loved her, of course."

She gave him a look that said she couldn't believe he was so naive. "Five years, Franklin, of her locking her door to him every night?"

"Willie, how would you know a thing like that?" He prided himself on being well informed on many people, particularly his family, but this he had never heard.

"Daughters talk to mothers and mothers talk to friends."

"Five years?" Now that was fortitude.

She nodded and there remained a question in her eyes.

Realization dawned and Franklin understood her need. "Willie, dear, Hampton men don't leave their women. You are as stuck with me as Tiffany was with Wade."

Her eyes assured him he had answered her unspoken fears.

"Whether we lose him over this or not, I'll be at your side." Franklin removed his glasses and leaned forward. "Now, it's time we told him the whole truth."

Wilhelmina shook her head. "That would be a huge mistake. He'd never forgive us."

"Let's give him more credit than that. But even if you're right, it's time we accept the consequences for what we did."

#

Franklin and Wilhelmina drove to the office. She waited in the car while he entered the building. Inside his office, he opened his desk drawer and lifted out the document. He slid it into his briefcase and, telling Mary he might be out the rest of the day, returned to the car.

"You found it fast," Wilhelmina said.

"I've never moved it in all these years."

"Strange that Wade never asked to see it."

Franklin took a deep breath and nodded. "I lived in fear of that moment all through his law studies. One day lately, I happened into the reception area when a couple was asking Mary for an appointment with Wade to ask about annulment proceedings."

"No!"

"I steered them into my office telling them that was one of my specialties."

"I'm warning you, Franklin. We're going to lose him over this. And Tiffany's family? Her mother will never forgive us. She'll tell everyone, and I won't be able to show my face at another function."

Franklin turned into his son's driveway. "We did what we thought was best."

Wilhelmina sighed. "Unfortunately, Wade won't see it that way."

"Let me do the talking on this one."

"Gladly."

Nancy showed the Hampton's into the bright, round sunroom that filled the base of the Victorian turret. Wade sat in his pajamas finishing the last bite of toast from a late breakfast. He started to stand to greet them, but Franklin waved him back into his chair.

"May we?" At Wade's nod, he scooted a chair out from the white wicker table for Wilhelmina and sat across from her on Wade's other side. "We need to talk to you."

"Sounds serious." Wade pushed the plate away from him and leaned back in his chair.

"Kay left?" Franklin decided this was no time for small talk.

His son's eyes held fresh pain as he replied, "Saturday."

"Why didn't you stop her? You're still in love with her after all these years, if I'm not mistaken."

Wade scowled. "Why do you ask?"

Wilhelmina reached toward him saying, "Wade, dear," but at a glance from Franklin she pressed her lips together and lowered her hand to her lap.

Wade looked from her to his father and arched an eyebrow. Franklin knew his newfound assertiveness would be strange to them all. About time I took charge, he thought.

Nancy came to the room carrying a tray with glasses of orange juice. Franklin tried to hide his exasperation at the interruption, but must not have succeeded because she set the tray down on the table without a word and disappeared to the kitchen.

"I know it sounds like we are prying into your business, but humor us, please. It's important."

Wade crossed his arms, which Franklin did not take as a promising sign.

"Kay has gone back to Spokane to pursue a medical degree. I told you about that yesterday, Dad, when I suspected you were the anonymous benefactor. She feels it's a calling from God that she can't disregard. I didn't have the right to ask her to stay."

"Why?" Franklin knew he was pushing his son's patience, but he had his reasons.

"If she's accepted, and I have no doubt she will be, she'll need to devote years to her studies. And she doesn't want to risk that my interest in her is a result of grief. Or loneliness. Or some kind of rebound effect. We'd need time to let our relationship grow. With me here and Kay who-knows-where, we don't have the time."

"You didn't ask her to stay?"

"We talked about her staying here until she's accepted to med school. She thinks people would be hurt if we... spent time together... so soon after Tiffany's death."

Wilhelmina nodded her head, and Franklin wondered about the wisdom of bringing her with him. He decided to change tactics.

"Wade, do you love your work?"

It took a moment for Wade to follow this new line of questioning. Good, Franklin thought, keep him off balance a bit. He watched his son's face as he obviously considered his words carefully.

Impatient, Franklin answered for him. "Wade, you are a peacemaker. You excel when you counsel clients toward compromise or resolution. It's obvious you enjoy that. But when you are representing someone in a win/lose situation, your heart isn't in your work."

Wade's scowl returned. "I didn't realize I was such a disappointment to you."

"Nothing's further from the truth. Your mother and I couldn't be prouder of you. When we thought we might lose you, we were devastated. Then along came Kay, and Dana, and Drew, willing to sacrifice everything for you. They put us to shame."

Franklin stalled for thinking time as he shifted his gaze from Wilhelmina to Wade, deciding how to proceed. He nodded toward Wilhelmina. "Your mother realized it before me, but we've been selfishly keeping you close ever since... ever since the day of your sister's funeral. The same day you backed down to keep the peace, rather than follow your heart."

Wade's features softened and he nodded.

Franklin continued. "Your mother wanted to show her gratitude to Kay, but doubted Kay would ever trust her enough to accept her gift."

Wade sat up. "You're the anonymous donor?"

Franklin didn't think he had ever seen his son sneer before.

"Right, a gift. Be honest, Mother. You've forced us apart again, like you did before. I should have guessed." Wade put his hands on the table to push himself out of the chair, but Franklin stopped him with a touch.

"Please, let us finish. There's more."

Wade sat, but crossed his arms again.

"Tiffany wasn't your wife."

Wade's eyes flashed wide, then narrowed. His voice dropped to a threatening whisper. "What did you say?"

Franklin presented the document from his briefcase. Wade looked at his own signature, smeared by Kay's tear. The annulment papers. Franklin could tell the papers hit his son with the full force of shame, loss, and anger.

Wade pushed his father's hand away. "I don't want to see them!"

"You need to look carefully."

"Why?"

Unable to say the words, Franklin signaled to Wilhelmina, and she spoke quietly. "We never filed the papers. Your father drew them up, but wanted to wait and reason with you and Kay together. I knew that wouldn't work, so I convinced you to sign them to give us time to adjust to losing one child before losing another. Then I took them to Kay. Even though she saw your signature, she wouldn't sign. But I did get her signature on our contract to pay her for not contacting you. She took my money and left. I copied her signature onto the annulment."

"You forged her signature?"

"It was stupid. We couldn't have the signature notarized, and your father made me realize we couldn't file the annulment. But we let you think we had, hoping no one would check on your Idaho marriage. Kay is and has been your wife, all along."

Wade's mind must have taken a moment to register all that his mother said. But when it did, he shoved the wicker table forward. The table leg hit Franklin's shoe and the table tipped, dumping plates, tray, and orange juice glasses all to the floor. Wilhelmina gasped and leapt out of her chair. Franklin jumped to stand between his wife and son.

Nancy hurried into the room, took a look at the three, and propped her fists on her hips.

Wilhelmina grabbed Wade's sleeve. "We were horribly wrong. We are terribly, terribly sorry. Please, forgive us."

Wade's words struggled through clenched teeth. "Mother, you need to find another ride home. Dad, you'll be driving me to Spokane as soon as I can get dressed. I'm going to be with my wife."

Franklin nodded.

Against Nancy's protest, her patient packed a bag. Wade apologized to her as she handed him his medications. "I'll pay you for the full two weeks we agreed on, but I have to go."

Nancy followed him toward the front door, but when she saw Wilhelmina bent over the broken glass and spilled juice, she hurried to help her.

Wade stopped and considered the women, caught between his need to make peace and his longing to be with Kay. He stood taller and stepped out the door. Behind him, he heard his mother's resolute voice.

"This is my mess, Nancy. I need to clean it up."

CHAPTER 22

In spite of his anger and desperation, Wade couldn't fault Franklin for his torturously slow driving over the icy pass that crossed the border between Montana and Idaho. But even when the roads improved as they neared Washington, the miles dragged by. When Franklin finally parked at the building that housed Kay's Spokane condo, Wade flew out of the car before his father even set the brake. His sudden move tugged at his sutures, but the pain barely registered.

Franklin called after him, "I'll get us a motel room. Call my cell phone."

Wade heard his father's car drive away while he began to hurry up the stairs outside Kay's condo. Halfway up, his body reminded him of the doctor's orders to avoid stairs. By the time he made it to the top of the flight his strength gave out.

He couldn't believe it. This close to Kay and he had no choice but to sit on the top step, head resting on his forearms, and wait for his energy to return so he could make it to her door. Now he wished he hadn't sat down, because the idea of standing seemed more than he'd be able to manage.

Someone approached from behind. He scooted over so they could make it past him on the stairs.

Kay sat next to him. "This is an improvement. Neither of us is unconscious this time we meet. Though you don't look far from it."

Great. He'd come to sweep her off her feet and he couldn't even make it to his. "How'd you know I was here?" He still couldn't quite raise his dizzy head.

"I didn't. I was bringing another load to my car. I planned to leave tomorrow morning to come to you." She drew his arm around her and slipped her shoulder under it. "Want help? They mean it when they say no strenuous activity. That includes stairs."

He pushed to standing with her help and they made their way to her couch. When he finally was lying down he couldn't take his gaze off of her. Something new shone in her face. Strength. Confidence. Her pain was gone.

"You were coming to me?" he asked.

"Yes. I decided to fight for what I love, and I love you."

He wanted to grab her and crush her in an embrace that he'd never release. Instead he opened his arms.

Kay settled on the floor next to the couch, an awkward position for the hug they attempted. He groaned with frustration.

Kay jumped back. "Did I hurt you?"

He pulled her close again. "We've both been hurt. But if you'll let me, I'll follow you anywhere and make it up to you, as the husband I always should have been." His cheeks warmed at how rehearsed his words sounded. They were the mantra that had kept him sane during the 300-mile drive.

"Husband? Is that a proposal?" Her forehead wrinkled, and he could imagine the objections she was marshaling.

"Too late. Seems you and I are still married and always have been." He drew the annulment papers out of his jacket inner pocket and unfolded them. These were never legalized."

Kay looked from the papers, to Wade's face, and back again. Her eyes widened, then her brows knit together, then her face relaxed. He knew from his own reaction some of what she was feeling.

"I always wondered how they managed to get the annulment when I wouldn't sign. That's what convinced me a family of lawyers could do anything, even take custody of the twins." She whispered "My heart knew I was married."

"I think mine did, too. I'm sorry I stopped listening to it, but I will from now on."

Kay ripped the papers lengthwise and then crosswise twice more before tossing them over her shoulder. Grinning at Wade, she reached out her arms to him and he enveloped her with love. Their lips met and through that first tentative—then suddenly eager—kiss, he traveled back in time to their wedding night. He trembled.

The movement frightened Kay. "Wade, you've had major surgery. You're worn out. You should sleep."

Actually, going to bed was precisely what he had in mind, but first he reached into another pocket. "Kay, I wanted to give you this, years ago. It's time you stopped wearing a wedding band you had to buy yourself."

She looked at the small jewelry box and then at him. He loved the way her eyes brightened. The spark that lit them. The grin that followed. She took it from him carefully and opened it.

"Wade, it's beautiful! How long have you had this?"

"I bought it the day you left Butte. Carried it all over Montana looking for you."

"And you kept it all these years?"

He took the ring from the box and inspected it. "An engagement solitaire didn't seem right since we were already married. The jeweler said these little diamonds all around the band signify eternity. That's how long I'll be yours, if you're willing to remain my wife."

Kay's kiss answered his question. He removed the ring she had bought and slid the new band over her finger.

"For better, for worse," they said together.

He leaned in for another kiss.

"Wait." She flattened her hand against his chest. "How did you get here? You shouldn't be driving yet."

Wade forced his mind away from where it had wandered. "I insisted my father drive me here as soon as he admitted we were still married. He's gone to a motel. We'll call him later."

The beloved soft gentleness had left Kay's face, replaced by the same stern look as Nancy, his nurse. "I'm glad you didn't drive. Between the pain medication and your incision you wouldn't have been safe on the road."

"You're right. I would have had a dozen speeding tickets between Butte and here. I thought my father was trying to make me crazy by following the speed limit." He kissed her again.

She drew back. The look of concern in her eyes made him want to hold her and never let her go.

"You know you aren't allowed to make love for at least three more weeks, don't you?"

He groaned. A definite disadvantage to having a nurse for a wife. Wade exhaled slowly to control himself. He had already waited too long, but he could be a patient man. He'd proven that over the years with Tiffany.

"But we can snuggle." Her naughty grin nearly did him in.

After a twin-bed nap spent curled around his Kay, Wade called his father to let him know he wouldn't need to be picked up. Before saying goodbye, his voice grew gentle. "Dad, thank you for being honest. Will Mother be all right?"

"Yes. This time she knows you'll be happy. That's all she ever wanted." He laughed. "That and grandchildren."

Grandchildren. The thought of having another baby with Kay—of being there for every moment of raising a child together—expanded Wade's chest with emotion. But would that be fair? Kay had already struggled her way through school once with infants. Ask her to be pregnant while in medical school? No, he couldn't. But she'd be over forty by the time she finished and the risks of a pregnancy then...

#

The next day, Franklin Hampton drove the final miles to his home dreading his arrival. What state would Wilhelmina be in? The last he'd seen her, she was bent over spilled orange juice in Wade's house. She might be nursing any number of moods: distraught about the disaster of their admission to their son and his furious reaction, frightened that they might have lost his love, disapproving of his return to Kay, or angry with Franklin for deciding they should tell him and then driving him to Spokane. Since it wasn't even noon yet, he hoped she wouldn't be numbing whichever mood with her favorite "little cocktail."

He drove into the garage. Her car was there. He opened the door into the mudroom and listened. Classical music played softly from somewhere upstairs. Not a bad sign. In her worst moods, she played angry-woman country songs. On her migraine days, no music at all would greet him. If the house were silent, he'd whisper his greeting into a darkened bedroom and she'd answer him with a groan. Mozart gave him hope as he climbed the stairs.

The music emanated not from the master bedroom, but from Sharon's old room. He opened the door and stopped dumbfounded. All the furniture crowded the center of the room and Wilhelmina stood, paintbrush in hand, with a lovely smear of light green across one cheek, the same color that now adorned previously peach walls.

"Hi Dear. Welcome back," she said. "Dana mentioned sea foam green being her favorite color. What do you think?" Pride straightened her shoulders and brightened her eyes.

Of all the moods he had prepared himself to endure, this middle-of-a-project excitement never occurred to him. Still trying to recover from the shock of Wilhelmina releasing this shrine-to-Sharon, he moved into the room and turned slowly around before proclaiming, "It's almost as beautiful as you are, Willie."

She leaned close to him but held the paintbrush away as she kissed him on the cheek. "I'm glad you like it. I think it was time to let go, don't you?"

He knew he must have a silly grin on his face, so he tried to pull himself together. "I've never seen you paint before. All these years I could have saved a fortune on decorators."

"I wanted to do it myself. For Dana. And I want to set up a room for Drew with dark woods and something military. Not camouflage, that's too obvious. Not airplanes, that's what I would have done when he was a boy." With that her face crumpled, her brave enthusiasm gone in an instant. "Oh Franklin, we missed so much and it was all my fault." She dropped the brush into the paint can and sank onto the bed.

Franklin joined her and drew her close, wrapping his arm around a shoulder that now trembled with emotion. She laid her head against him and he rocked her a bit while she sniffed away tears.

In a moment, she wiped her cheeks and discovered the paint her tears had moistened. He handed her his handkerchief but she simply crumpled it in a ball.

"Why did I buy her off, demand that she not see our son again? We could have been there for all the milestones the twins accomplished. We missed cutting teeth and first steps and potty training and learning to pump a swing and ride a bike and kindergarten and... everything!" She wiped away more tears and the handkerchief came away green but she didn't seem to notice. This was not the appearance-conscious wife he left yesterday.

She wore the frightened expression of a defendant who did and didn't want to know the jury's verdict. "How is Wade? Will he forgive us?" She swallowed. "Will we ever see him again?"

There it was. The fear that held them both. The possibility they probably deserved. The prospect that made him inhale sharply before he answered, trying to reassure them both. "He'll come around. It may take time but I have to believe his anger will pass. He did ask me if you'd be ok."

"I've told God and I'll tell Wade—if he gives me the chance—I swear I'll never be controlling again."

The mention of God surprised Franklin even more than walking into this *sea foam* room. Since the day Sharon died, Wilhelmina had turned her back on God. Oh, not in a way obvious to anyone else. She still attended service every Sunday and chaired the church fundraisers, but she wouldn't pray with him at night anymore and her Bible hadn't been touched in all these years.

He answered carefully. "We need to place this in God's hands, then. Let's trust He'll do a better job of managing our lives than we've done."

CHAPTER 23

Between learning that Wade's mother was the anonymous benefactor and discovering she was still married to him, Kay felt like she had lost her path. Medical school no longer seemed an obvious choice, but she studied whenever he napped. He still needed bed rest, and Kay didn't take much convincing to join him. They talked late into the nights and slept until mid-mornings, but she made sure they ate regularly and she maintained careful watch on his insulin levels. Wade didn't ask what the future would hold for them.

On Saturday, she left him to take the admission tests for medical school. Her heart wanted to stay home with him, but her mind had controlled her heart for years. She would take the test and make decisions later.

By Sunday, Wade had convinced Kay he felt well enough to accompany her to church. They entered holding hands, and Kay fought giddiness as she scooted into the pew beside Brenda. She wished she had a camera to record the look on her friend's face when she saw Wade. Kay couldn't resist; she wiggled the fingers of her sparkly left hand. Brenda's eyes bulged, and Kay had to stifle a laugh.

When the minister invited people to introduce themselves to those sitting near them, Kay said the words she thought she would never be able to say, "Let me introduce you to my husband, Wade Hampton."

Brenda sat speechless, so Kay continued, "Wade, this is my dearest friend, Brenda Potter."

As Brenda found her voice and began, "It's about time—" the minister started a prayer. Kay laughed to see Brenda so flummoxed.

When they stepped out of the church, the wind howled around them. Kay raised her voice, "Come to breakfast and we'll tell you all about it!"

147

While Kay prepared the griddle and batter for pancakes, she made Wade rest on the sofa. She wished she could hear the conversation as two of her favorite people became acquainted, but she could tell by their voices that they didn't need her. When she called them to breakfast, Brenda moved right to the point.

"What does this mean for your chance at being a doctor?"

Wade look equally as anxious to know what might lie ahead.

She replied, "I was hoping we all could spend some prayer time this morning and see if we can figure that out."

The three held hands at the table and asked for God's blessing on the food and help in discerning His will.

Brenda was a terrier that wouldn't let go. "Do you still want to go to med school?"

Wade's fork stopped in midair.

Kay took her time to answer. "I've always dreamed of being a doctor. But right now, when the chance to fulfill it hovers within my grasp, I'm not so sure."

Brenda leaned back in her chair. "Ok, let's backtrack. How has God been working in your life lately?"

"I think it started with your Jubilee quote."

"That's right. Where I heard 'celebrate,' you heard, 'go home.'"

"Precisely what I didn't ever want to do."

Wade lifted her hand and kissed it. "Thank God you did."

Brenda persisted. "Have there been other scripture passages that spoke to you?"

Kay tipped her head to one side. "A sermon, actually. My mother's minister spoke about the Sabbath and how we need to rely on God. How He wants to nurture us."

Brenda nodded. "You've always been the nurturer. I knew something was different last week when you asked to come over and let me host you. That was the first time you didn't insist on feeding me at your house."

"So on the one hand," Kay squeezed Wade's hand, "our nurturing God brought me to my mother when she needed me and to Wade when he needed me. He almost died!"

Wade wiped his mouth on his napkin. "God does seem to have perfect timing."

Brenda nodded, "And on the other?"

Kay lifted her other hand. "Wade's mother, who had never wanted us together, offered to put me through med school. Might be God's inspiration. Wade says she seems sincere in wanting to do this in appreciation for saving her son—"

"And providing her with the coveted grandchildren," Wade interrupted.

"But if Wade stays with me while I study to be a doctor, he has to leave his law practice behind."

Brenda turned to Wade. "How do you feel about that?"

Kay thought Brenda had missed her calling in not becoming a therapist.

Wade rumbled his throat. "We're trying to be completely honest with each other." He checked with Kay and she nodded him on. "I thought I didn't like my work. I hate the idea of winners and losers. But I love Butte and the people there. I think I'd miss helping them."

"You could help people somewhere else, or back in Butte after med school," said Brenda.

"I certainly would choose Kay over Butte," Wade hurried his words. "But we're expressing our preferences."

Brenda turned to Kay, "What are your preferences?"

"I want it all!"

The three laughed.

"What would be better about being a doctor, rather than a nurse?" asked Brenda.

The question stunned Kay. Weren't the benefits obvious? People who were smart enough to be doctors should be doctors. A sudden realization made her chin drop. She whispered, "Pride."

Brenda and Wade both stopped chewing.

Kay nodded. "I'm ashamed to say it, especially after all these years of nursing. I think I'd be more proud of myself as a doctor."

"Why?" both asked.

"They're admired. They make more money. People respect their accomplishments." She covered her mouth with her hand. "That can't be it, can it? I want to be a doctor to help people, but, I do that now, and with closer contact with the patients than I'd have as a doctor."

Brenda offered, "There'd be the challenge of diagnosis."

"Maybe I'd enjoy that out of pride, too." After a pause, she felt a wide grin spread across her face. "I like being a nurse! I don't need to be a doctor."

She glanced from Wade to Brenda and back again. Their faces weren't judgmental or disapproving. They appeared rather self-satisfied, actually.

Brenda pointed her fork toward Kay. "Be patient," she admonished. "Sit with this discovery a while and see if it feels right. I think you'll know for sure in God's time." She took another bite.

But later that night, Kay didn't feel God's peace. She knew she could please Wade by moving back to Butte and work as a nurse. He hadn't said anything about children, but the possibility of another baby tantalized her. They could raise this child together. And yet, she wanted to grow in her career, too. Having been offered the chance to be a doctor had stirred a longing for a new challenge.

As if living with a husband and considering another baby weren't challenge enough, she chided herself.

What direction does God want me to travel? Why is it so hard to know?

#

Wade and Kay prayed together about their life decisions, but Kay seemed even more confused. Wade, for his part, believed they were meant to return to Butte, but he would go wherever Kay decided. He could study for the bar exam in a new state and be working again before long.

He found himself distracted by the children in the condo complex and in church. Kay had missed out on being a doctor, but he had missed being a father. He wanted to jiggle and comfort his own little one, to stand proudly with his baby in his arms.

A few weeks passed without a decision, but time caught up with them. Kay was away attending Brenda's Jubilee party when Wade's secretary, Mary, called.

"Your father told me not to bother you with work details, Mr. Wade, but I thought I should remind you of your doctor appointment at 3:00 on Friday."

"I'd forgotten, Mary. Thank you."

"Should I reschedule it?"

"No, I'll be there." He thought of Kay, who had enchanted him only minutes ago when she donned a flowery hat after brushing her hair, the hair he loved running his fingers through. He looked forward to that appointment and the permission for *light activity* that should come with it.

#

Kay had grudgingly accepted that Wade could survive if she left him for a few hours. Though she worried as she drove away from the condo, she brightened at the thought of attending Brenda's Jubilee celebration. The same Bible phrase that had dragged her home in September hadn't dimmed its excitement for her dear friend. The subject filled most of Brenda's conversation.

Her friend threw open the door before she could knock, and Kay thought if Brenda had a tail, it would be wagging the woman's whole body. They hugged and Kay held up her apron. "I'm here. Put me to work!"

However, though she had arrived an hour before party time, everything appeared ready. To the right of the entry, a table stretched to fill the dining room. On a lace-topped blue tablecloth, china place settings invited her forward. Each had a place card with a guest's name and a quality. Kay caught Brenda's excitement and could hardly wait to see where she would sit. "Where's mine?"

Brenda pointed and Kay read her own name and the word *Hospitality*. She looked at Brenda and cocked her head.

Brenda laughed. "Each of my friends has taught me something from their strengths. You've always hosted me so nicely, and I let you. We were a perfect match because you didn't ever want to come to my house and, secretly I didn't want you here."

The words left Kay confused.

"Kay, I'm a hoarder. I have been since my husband died, though it worsened with each child who left the nest. Until you came to tea when you arrived back in town, nobody had been in my house for at least six years. There weren't even cleared paths from room to room. Thankfully, the one time you finally invited yourself over here, I was ready. You will never know how good it felt to welcome you in and not be ashamed."

A hoarder? No way. Kay studied the room. Only a vase of flowers or a bowl of party treats adorned each shiny surface.

"When I read that Jubilee verse, I wasn't completely honest with you. Yes, I heard celebrate, but part of my joy was the realization that I could, with God's help, end my slavery to stuff. Every corner of my house held valuable, meaningful treasures that, when I started liberating myself of the slavery, actually amounted to magazines and shopping bags with forgotten gifts or projects, piles of papers, and things I probably wouldn't ever *need* someday."

Kay turned slowly around. From this festive room she could see a clean-as-an-ER kitchen. Beyond it, she glimpsed another table decorated like the one she stood near. She smiled at her friend, who seemed to be basking in well-deserved pride.

"I've always heard hoarding is one of the hardest anxieties to overcome. How did you manage?"

"One square foot at a time. Knowing a little about the life-fears you went home to face, I decided I could brave my demons, too. I 'proclaimed liberty throughout the land,' and then I took a deep breath and pursued help wherever I could find it. I met regularly with an experienced counselor, started some medication, and prayed constantly!

"Talking to God kept me going, and with the image of my friends surrounding me around a table that I hadn't seen the top of in years, I was determined to sort through this one room." She motioned around the dining area. "This is just how I imagined it. Success in one room led me to the next. I think the neighbors started to worry a dumpster in my driveway was going to be permanent yard décor."

Kay couldn't quite picture the chaos Brenda described, but she looked again at the table with its luncheon plates, cloth napkins, silverware, crystal glasses, and tea cups. Two cups and saucers adorned each setting, one for tea and one overflowing with party favors. She lifted the latter, saucer and all. It nestled chocolates, silken teabags, a small crocheted magnet teapot, and a demitasse silver spoon, all protected with iridescent plastic wrap and tied with a ribbon. The favor cups didn't match, but rather each was unique and lovely.

"When a room emerged from its muddle, I rewarded myself by allowing time to scour garage sales and thrift stores to collect cups so each guest could take home a memory."

Kay felt like a child at the most magical birthday party she'd ever attended. She set the cup down and hugged her friend. "I'm so proud of you!"

"Thanks," Brenda answered with a grin, "but we still have lots to do. I'll hand you plates of the cutest little sandwiches you've ever seen, and you place them on the tables. Then we'll start the tea kettles boiling. Would you mind stirring some lemon and sugar into the ice tea? It's in the refrigerator..."

They hurried together and felt ready only a moment before the doorbell began to ring. As guests entered, Kay would carry coats to a spotlessly clean and almost bare looking bedroom. Brenda would introduce her friends to each other, but Kay had given up remembering names. She didn't worry because Brenda had a name tag ready for each woman, complete with the lesson or virtue she'd learned from that friend. With the magnet-attached tags (Brenda didn't want pins to hurt anyone's clothing), Kay and the others would easily be reminded of the name and also be able to ask about the quality word as a conversation starter.

Two women about Kay's age arrived breathless and apologizing for being late. They stopped in the entry with amazement on their faces as they took in the beauty of the rooms they could see. Brenda proudly introduced them to all as her daughters. As everyone began to take their places at one of the two large tables, Kay intended to begin distributing filled teapots but the daughters insisted on Kay and Brenda sitting while they served. Kay could see their mother in the girls, and the way they doted on her guests testified to how they'd been raised.

She watched Brenda turn from friend to friend, chattering and receiving their compliments with shining eyes. After a short time, Brenda excused herself and made her way to the other table to visit with more of the influential women of her life. There were easily 30 present, which made Kay wonder how many people she could celebrate as friends and mentors. She had to admit that, only months ago, she wouldn't have been able to name more than a handful, but now she could add Francie, and Madge and Agnes, her mother's friends, and of course, Sadie herself.

Kay's mind drifted to thoughts of those good women of Butte. She imagined them around a table like this, guests of honor as part of both her past and her future. She wanted to host something like this for them, but she didn't want to wait until she was a Jubilee woman of 50. A slow smile lifted her cheeks and suddenly she was looking around the room through misty eyes. She knew what she wanted.

A wedding.

And a wedding reception to include and thank the people she loved most. She could hardly wait to get home to talk to Wade!

CHAPTER 24

Wade didn't even wait for Kay to remove her hat before he told her about the call.

"Time to get you back to Butte for your post-op," she replied. "With any luck, you'll be cleared for moderate activity." Her wicked grin returned.

Wade lunged for her and she dodged. "Sorry, no. Not yet. We'll need to make this memorable."

"Oh believe me, I'll never forget—"

"Wade, I've been thinking." Kay sounded hesitant.

He sobered. "No second thoughts, I hope."

She shook her head slowly, and seemed distracted. "We need a wedding."

"But we're married."

"We're married legally. I want to acknowledge our union spiritually."

Wade squinted with confusion as the subject jumped from weddings to Brenda's Jubilee celebration. Kay's words now came rapid-fire. "The love and support for Brenda was so strong it almost pulsated in her house…"

He struggled not to glaze over like he used to when his mother and Tiffany began talking fundraiser chatter. Kay was caught up in the same fervor. He heard, "Formal tea…," and, "Brenda made us feel cherished," but nearly hit overload at the mention of "teacup favors, chocolate dipped strawberries, finger sandwiches and petit fours," whatever those were.

Kay must have noticed his bewilderment. She slowed her words and took his hands in hers. "God's Spirit was at the party. I want that. I want

Him to be Director of our new life."

Wade took a deep breath. Yes, this he could understand.

Kay gazed into his eyes with such intensity that he had to blink and swallow. She continued, "We need our children and our parents around us. And a minister to bless our vows. Our marriage needs to be supported by a worship community. Then it will feel right to have our honeymoon."

Wade saw flowers and musicians and a catered reception in his future. His mother would be in her glory. But how long would this all take? He'd waited way too long already. "When?" The word came out as a croak.

"Thanksgiving weekend!" Kay's face glowed with anticipation and his heart melted once again.

"You want a ceremony in two weeks?" Yes, he could wait that long; he could wait forever if Kay would be his. But two weeks sounded much better than forever.

"Dana will be home. I doubt we'll get Drew home, but it's worth a try. At my mother's church. Only family. And Brenda. Oh, and Francie."

Wade had observed his mother in similar mode when she'd been struck by inspiration for a new project. He nodded and followed his father's lead. He'd go with the flow.

"So where will the reception be, Mrs. Hampton? And the honeymoon?"

"How about both in a beautiful Victorian? I've always dreamed of sleeping in a turret." She laid her hand on his heart. "Let's go home, Wade."

She couldn't have made him happier.

#

Kay rose early and packed the car while Wade slept. After a light breakfast, they left and drove east toward Montana. When Kay declared it time for lunch, they were near the little town in Idaho where they had been married. She drove through for fast food and he complained when she insisted his French fry days were over. They shared kisses and salads in the now vacant lot where their first married night had been spent in a motel long gone.

At a rest stop, as Kay returned to the car, Wade closed his cell phone and said he had confirmed the doctor appointment.

Three hours later, they drove into Butte and straight to his house. They parked in the garage, and when Kay opened her car door, she inhaled the aroma of fresh lumber. "I love that smell. Where's it coming from?"

Wade responded by guiding her through a door. A full woodworking shop adjoined the garage and he proudly showed her several pieces of furniture waiting in various stages for his completion. Their style reminded her of the desk in his office and the little writing table Wilhelmina said he made.

"These are beautiful! You are as much an artist as my dad was!"

Kay loved the pride that showed in his face as she admired his work.

"This was what filled my time and saved my sanity over the years. Come see more. The house is full of things I made."

He made as if to carry Kay over the threshold, but she refused. "I wouldn't want any strained sutures to spoil my honeymoon."

Wade toured Kay through his Victorian home. She had visited him on the ground floor, so had caught glimpses of the living room and the turret sunroom when Nancy led her to visit Wade in the guest bedroom. As much as she loved it at that time, she had thought of the house as Tiffany's. Now she focused instead on the furniture and the fine carpentry in the crown moldings, mantles, and staircase.

When they climbed the stairs, Wade took her to his master bedroom that included the turret, where a seating arrangement surrounded with books called to her. Creams and browns softened the light in the room and impressed on her a sense of masculinity. She resisted the longing inspired by the dark cherry four-poster bed with its carved headboard.

"This was my room," Wade said.

She noted that he didn't say, "our room," but she kept the thought to herself.

He led her back to the hallway and opened a second door. "This was Tiffany's." Kay took in the paisley pink room and then turned to her husband.

"Yes, we had separate rooms. Tiffany asked me to move out five years ago after her first heart attack. After time went by without her changing her mind, I combined two smaller rooms and added a bathroom for myself."

"Two master bedrooms?"

"Unless you are a fan of pink swirls, I think mine is the better of the two."

Kay had to admit she had found her dream home. Tiffany had lived here, but the memories she left behind would not come between Kay and Wade. "Yours is the one I want to share."

"You're sure, Kay? Moving back to Butte is what you want?"

His smile lighted his eyes and Kay had the momentary impression she had glimpsed his soul. She'd sacrifice anything for him. She'd make this marriage—and God willing, a baby—enough of a new challenge.

She looked around her. Yes, she would share his room where Tiffany had never slept. The paisley room could make a fine nursery, with a little work. And less wallpaper.

Two more bedrooms filled a third floor with plenty of room for Drew and Dana whenever they wanted to spend time with their parents. She followed Wade back to his room and then up a narrow staircase into the top floor of the turret. In the center of the little round room stood an easel. Stretched canvases waited under one of the six windows. Kay hurried to inspect a small set of drawers and found each held tubes of acrylic pigments. A paint shirt dangled from a hook between two of the windows. A column of wooden cups hung between two other windows and held a variety of brushes.

"Happy housewarming, Kay." Wade rocked a bit on the balls of his feet. He seemed to be taking as much pleasure in the room as Kay.

"Oh, Wade, this is perfect lighting! My own little studio! What fun! How did you arrange this?"

"I called my Dad from the rest stop and asked him to get it ready. He said he'd talk to your mother to see what you'd need."

"Wade, if I'm not mistaken, these are my dad's easel and brushes. What a wonderful gift, from you and my mom! Dad, too, I guess."

#

Kay and Wade took their parents out to dinner that night and told them they would be staying in Butte. Kay watched her in-laws' reaction and was relieved to see true pleasure.

When Wilhelmina excused herself to freshen up in the restroom, Kay joined her. "I wanted to thank you personally, Wilhelmina, for your offer of medical school. Wade and I have been praying over the decision and believe it isn't in God's plan for us right now."

Wilhelmina nodded. "We'll keep the money in an account for Dana's schooling, if you don't use it."

Kay hugged the woman who hardly seemed the villain she had believed her to be for so many years. "I'd like to ask you for something else, too."

Wilhelmina raised an eyebrow.

"Could you help me and my mother pull together a wedding a week from Saturday?"

The animation that lit Wilhelmina's face marked Kay's plunge into a swift, unrelenting current. She and Sadie hung on for dear life as Wilhelmina guided them smoothly past six months' worth of rocky rapids in only ten days.

A second, slower current drew her in at Wade's postoperative appointment. His doctor apologized for keeping them waiting an hour. "I'm sorry, we're understaffed lately."

Wade introduced Kay. "My wife might be looking for a nursing position."

The doctor acknowledged her with a nod and handshake. "What this area especially needs are physician assistants. Have you considered extending your training in that direction?"

Kay felt an adrenaline jolt that reminded her of Brenda's words, "Kay, sometimes we realize a message is meant for us because it brings a sense of joy."

A Physician Assistant program in Bozeman was within commuting distance. She could be trained to diagnose and prescribe, working under the supervision of a physician. The idea took hold in Kay's heart and she knew without a doubt that this was God's leading.

However, first she had a wedding to attend. Kay realized Wilhelmina would have preferred more elegance, but the short notice, and a surprising acquiescence on Wilhelmina's part, helped simplicity win out. Francie styled the bride's hair, and stood with Brenda as her attendants. Kay had been thrilled when Francie asked her to add Allen and their girls to the guest list. Dana beamed as maid of honor and Drew flew in to be best man. He would need to catch the next flight out, but his presence completed the perfection of the day for Kay.

Kay and Wade followed their attendants up the aisle. Before they joined Francie, Brenda, Dana, and Drew in front of the altar, they turned to their parents for the first of many congratulatory hugs. Sadie glowed as mother of the bride, and Wilhelmina apologized for her tears of happiness as she kissed Kay.

The minister waited until Kay and Wade had taken their places on the altar where their attendants stood. His first reading had been Kay's choice and she delighted in how differently it settled into her soul today.

"Consecrate the fiftieth year and proclaim liberty throughout the land to all its inhabitants. It shall be a jubilee for you; each one of you is to return to his family property and each to his own clan."

She had fought God's leading to return home, but now her heart surged with gratitude for that push. She had returned to her own clan, a larger family than she left, and one that now included the love of her life and his family. Three months earlier she never would have thought it all possible, but then, anything is possible with God.

After a short sermon on enduring love and the importance of family interdependence, the minister rose a bit on his toes and said, "Whenever I celebrate a renewal of vows I ask any married couples in the congregation to stand if they'd like to renew their own." Franklin rose and guided Wilhelmina to join him. Then Allen Shea stood and approached the altar to take Francie's hand. He led her over to join their daughters, faced her, and took both her hands in his. He nodded at the minister. Then Kay and Wade, along with Franklin and Wilhelmina, and Francie and Allen filled in their own names as they repeated after the minister, "I ____, receive you, ____, to be my lawfully wedded spouse. I will love, honor, and cherish you, for better, for worse, for richer, for poorer, in sickness and in health, every day of my life." Though Kay knew she beamed with happiness, tears of joy streamed down both Francie and Allen's faces.

Kay and Wade shed tears of their own later that night, as they shared completely the love that had endured their long separation.

#

A month later, Kay lit two holly-ringed red candles on the grand table in the dining room of the Victorian house that had become very much her home. She sat and, as Wade led grace aloud, she silently prayed a blessing for each face around her Christmas table: her mother, her daughter, her husband and his parents. Enthusiasm animated Dana's face whenever she talked about her classes. Drew's phone call that morning had satisfied her that he was healthy and excited about his work. Kay missed her children daily, but knowing they followed their dreams made it endurable.

Wade squeezed her hand under the table. She added another silent prayer of thanksgiving. He continued to look healthier each day with no signs of organ rejection. It had turned out that he would be the one starting classes soon. A mediation training program suited him perfectly and he looked forward to working with businesses and individuals to reach agreements beneficial to all. In the meantime, while Kay dabbled with painting an animal mural on the wall of the bedroom near theirs, he was crafting the most beautiful cradle she had ever seen.

Kay resisted resting her hand on her stomach. Yesterday they had confirmed a new Hampton would join them by summer's end, but that news would wait for Wade to announce with a toast over dessert. She had decided to postpone beginning the Physician Assistant program. She wanted to fully enjoy this little one's beginnings in all the ways she hadn't been able to with the twins.

Wade stood and lifted a glass of sparkling cider. Dessert was still two courses away, but he obviously couldn't wait. "Let's raise our glasses in thanksgiving for God's Steadfast Love!" Then he turned and lifted his glass to Kay. "And to new life!"

The room fell silent, but only until Kay nodded. Then love cheered.

EPILOGUE

Kay hugged her daughter to her chest and gazed beyond her at the college campus. Two short years ago Kay had been leaving Dana at school. Now one-year-old Sharon Stuart Hampton wriggled and leaned with outstretched arms to her father. Wade swung her up onto his shoulders.

Kay turned to them. "See Mama's school, Sherrie? Before we know it we'll be dropping you off at a college."

"Or, if we're lucky—" Wade said as he lifted his chin to see Sherrie above him, "you'll be like your mom and commute so we get more years with you."

Sherrie drooled a wet grin and Wade swung her over his head and back into his arms in time to avoid a wet forehead.

He faced Kay and the tenderness in his eyes brought moisture to Kay's. After cradling the baby with his left arm, he brushed away a joy-tear from Kay's cheek with his right hand. "Are you worried about leaving her during the days?"

"Not at all. Between your mother and mine, not to mention her doting father, I'm only afraid she'll be spoiled."

"Count on it. We can all hardly wait until next week when you start classes. Now go buy the books you need and we'll play here in the shade until you get back."

Kay opened the door to the bookstore, ready to conquer a new world, but glanced back before it closed. Wade waved their daughter's little hand and Kay knew their vow would never be broken again.

The End

ABOUT THE AUTHOR

Betty Arrigotti was born and raised in Anaconda, Montana, not far from where her characters grew up. She moved to Spokane, Washington for college like her heroine, but then marriage called her farther west to Portland, Oregon. As her four daughters flew the nest, she began a second career by studying counseling, spiritual direction, and writing. With this third novel, she has hit her creative stride. However, like Kay, faith and family still take precedence and keep her balanced and busy.

Made in the USA
San Bernardino, CA
25 April 2015